SCENT

of the

WILD

SCENT of the WILD

a novel

Andi Gregory Pearson

To Madeleine —
Keep writing!
Best wishes for
creativity and
success —
Andi
2018

Scent of the Wild

Library of Congress Cataloging-in-Publication Data

Pearson, Andi Gregory.
Scent of the Wild: a novel / by Andi Gregory Pearson
p. cm.
ISBN-13: 978-1-4951-5771-4

Published in the United States of America

Cover design: Sydney Smith
Interior design: F. H. Spock & Associates

In memory of my father and
in honor of my dear
sweet family

I half expect to see you
fill the autumn air
like breath —

Kevin Young

Chapter One

IN THE YEARS BEFORE SHE LEFT US, the story of how my mother met my father – how our family was formed and later fractured, splintered, wrecked beyond repair – had been told many times. Before I was eight, I knew the saga, well, most of it. And I think the 742 residents of MacKremmon, Colorado, had heard the story, too. Small town gossip dies soap-opera slow and the story of how Edie Dawson, who wasn't yet my mother, had blown into town and guided her beat-up 1942 Plymouth into Mac's Garage where she met Chester Evans, who wasn't yet my father, was practically folklore.

Early one Wednesday morning she got out of the car, the account goes, struck a match on the scratchy border of the cardboard matchbook, held its flame to the tip of a cigarette firm between her lips and puffed life into the tobacco. She removed the cigarette, used her index finger and thumb to lift a tiny piece of tobacco from her tongue and asked Chester to take a look at the car. He'd stared at her, he said, through the drifting sulfurous haze, nodded as if it had fogged his brain, and walked slowly around the car. In the early 1950's, he was a mechanic, a good one, one that other car lovers called "a greaser." He had worked in the garage for years, could diagnose a jammed fuel line or a worn piston almost without looking.

Chester had just opened the garage and here was the first customer of the day. He looked down the front of Edie's car. The sleek black hood led to the grinning silver grill, an eager barrier to the lower car front. Under it, there should have been a front bumper. It was missing, that bumper, had left its spot, was gone. Without it, each fender perched protective but unsupported. Under each fender, a tire sat rigid and supple as a backbone, ready to roll quickly away.

Dirty red southwest road grime covered the black body like a spotty dropcloth and fingers of highway dust smeared themselves across the windows. Gritty, defiant smoke spurted up from the engine block of the two-door coupe as Chester lifted the black hood.

"Whew," Mama always wiped her forehead as she showed how he fanned the acrid-sweet smelling water-fog from his face and adjusted the hood prop gingerly.
"This radiator's about worn out," he told her. Daddy was tall, unbowed, young, and he had to bend to fit under the new space of the opened hood. "Didn't you notice a funny smell lately?" he'd asked.

"Smell? What kind of smell, honey?" She'd run her fingers through her hair and tilted her head to the right. A tendril of dark hair glided on dry morning breeze.

Mama said his index finger and thumb danced on the heated cap and as he unscrewed it just as the radiator spewed up angry water. Chester yanked himself out from under the hood and took two rapid steps back, away from the potential scald.

"Well, sometimes it can smell sticky sweet, like hot maple syrup." She said he took a deep inhale of clean air. "It's burning up. You must have driven all night. And I noticed you've got a Georgia license plate. You didn't drive this car all that way, did you?" She could tell he'd wanted to look at her and now was the time. He didn't just look, he narrowed his eyes as if he were trying to figure out the intricacies of womankind by scanning her facial details.

"Yeah," Edie gave a smushed laugh as she settled the pack of cigarettes in her right jeans pocket, "and the radiator wasn't the only thing that gave out on the trip." She winked at Chester. "Good thing I'm a gal who doesn't have to depend on some man to take care of me." She paused and then added, "Not that there's anything wrong with that."

Chester spent the next hour patching the car together. By then, the radiator had cooled enough for him to pour water from a green-glass Coke bottle into its remaining shards. Edie used the ladies' room, paced up and down in front of the nondescript station, fanned herself with a piece of accordion-folded newspaper and lit one cigarette after another. She talked almost nonstop.

Chester shook his head, took a fraying rag out of his hip pocket and wiped his hands. He held the greasy bit of cloth between his hand and the almost-pointed nose of the car. There was a sound of metal clanking against itself as he slammed the hood shut.

"These cars were made during the war and the original parts weren't always the best quality. It'll probably get you where you're going today, but I'm telling you this old buggy won't make it much longer," he said. "This car is eleven years old and it's gonna need new bushings, bearings and seals. Right now, she's running hotter than noontime in Denver." Chester wiped his hands again. He looked down at them to keep his eyes off Edie.

"That thing's hung together with bailin' wire and sealin' wax, sweetie." Edie tugged a tube of lipstick out of her left jeans pocket, popped the cover and ran bright red over both lips. "But it's all right. I'll bet you can keep it going for awhile." Her head tilted toward her left shoulder. "I figure that's about all I'll need.

Things change, you know."

Edie had asked for directions to Radium, twenty miles away.

"Radium?" Chester wondered aloud, "Nothing in Radium but livestock ranching."

"Yeah, I got a job waiting for me, cooking for the hands at the Beckwith Ranch. I'm a pretty good cook," she smiled. "You should taste my southern fried chicken sometime."

Chester could tell she was flirting with him and he felt a scratchy hopefulness. His local girlfriend had broken up with him and Edie's was the freshest face he'd seen in MacKremmon in awhile. As he watched, Edie got into the car and steered it onto the black asphalt road. Keeping her eyes on the road ahead and one hand on the Bakelite steering wheel, she stuck her entire left arm out of the car window. Daddy said her fingers waggled as if casting a magic spell.

The story goes on that while Chester kept up his routine of eating, sleeping and working on his treasured Chevy, he wondered if he'd ever see Edie again. But she got a ride from Radium, after the Plymouth did indeed go its last mile and turned up at the garage as a late August Friday slow-laned its way toward night.

Chester's jaw dropped in surprise as he came around the corner of the dull grey cement block building and saw Edie, casual up against his Chevrolet, the one he'd recently spent two hours polishing. Her left arm was held straight down at her side, hand holding a cigarette. Her right arm was bent at the elbow, so the fingers fluttered next to her face and drew Chester's attention.

He always said that he took one look and saw her in wrinkled jeans, a green plaid shirt under a faded denim jacket, a red bandana tied around her neck. His heart revved like an accelerator at a drag race. He was twisting his long, thin hands onto a clean garage rag and they froze for a few seconds. His eyes blinked rapidly while they adjusted to the brightness of her.

They went to Kate's Café on Highway 58, ordered cheeseburgers and sides and settled into the booth. Awkwardness was still in Chester but Edie chatted as if they'd known each other from sandbox days. Edie mashed her cigarette into an ashtray full of butts and ashes. Chester reached for the encrusted plastic ketchup bottle. She asked if Chester was his real name and he nodded.

"What?" she asked aghast, "Your mother actually named you *Chester*? What was she thinking? I never imagined there was a name worse than Edith. Well, it don't make no never mind." She took the ketchup bottle out of his hand, upended it and squirted the red slush onto her plate. She dipped a deep fried onion ring into it and took a noisy bite.

"As of right now, you're Chet and that's all there is to it." She brushed her hands together as if she'd just finished planting a seed or changing a tire.

Folks who knew him then said that unease had to work its way out of Chet while he got used to the new name. Chester was a family name, his mother's maiden name, the name his late parents had given him. But the tall, gawky twenty-four-year-old with the almost symmetrically round face, thick dark hair that grew up from a widow's peak in the middle of his forehead and intense dark eyes had only slept with two women – Heidi Brewster, who married Chet's best friend Jay Harmon and moved to Estes Park where they and their little one now lived in a mobile home, and a hooker he had met on a bachelor-bash trip to Denver.

A decisive new name seemed like it could be an advantage in lots of ways. In the following days, whenever he mentioned it to anyone in MacKremmon, their face would light up and reply, "*Chet*, yeah, it suits you!" Soon, the whole town called him by the new name – and saw him in a new light.

Every time he'd ever written his name, he'd thought that

Chester was a name that conveyed old-fashioned, boring, angular, all corners – it was the known, the everyday, the unexciting. *Chet* was the name of a man who was dashing, daring, rounded, sexy. So even though changing his name gave him a fleeting sense of cheating, a brief, jagged sense of disloyalty to the parents who had named him, *Chester* was left behind as he became *Chet*. It didn't take him long to grow into the name and to throw his shoulders back when he walked. Daddy said he felt his new self-confidence stuck out like a hood ornament on an old Packard.

Edie was three years older and she was always full of the chaos of blaring her own life-horn, as Daddy always put it. That year, 1953, the movie theatre in Grand Lake was only open in the summertime and this was the Saturday after Labor Day, the last night for the show.

In front of the Bijou, girls were reading the bold colored movie posters. One particular poster featured a shirtless Burt Lancaster waving a pirate's hat and swinging from a rope - *The Crimson Pirate* had been released last year but had just played in MacKremmon two weeks ago.

Some of the girls were admiring each other's outfits while the guys lined up at the curved glass window, buying tickets to tonight's film. Three of the girls wore sleek, elegant blouses in different colors, tucked into snugly fitting cotton skirts that zipped up the back. Two young women wore stylish Bermuda shorts, almost to the knees, with a sharp pleat ironed neatly down the front. And one bold brunette had on a crisp white shirt tucked into jet-black slacks that tapered down to the ankle, Audrey Hepburn style.

The Beckwith Ranch pick-up dropped hands off at various locations on Saturday night and Chet paced the sidewalk as he waited for it to screech up to the curb. Finally, it did and as Edie got out and slammed the door, long whistles and yells of "Have fun, Edie!" and "Go get'im, Edie!" were heard. As the truck skidded away, two girls in the crowd coughed from the dust clouds kicked up. Edie threw up her hand in a wave without looking back at the truck.

Edie's face showed an easy, satisfied grin and as she sashayed up to him, he saw she wore a puffy short skirt, bright orange, the color of tomato soup still in the can, dotted with large white polka dots. At a spot right of center, a piece of the skirt's hem had been stitched up about five inches, like a can-can dancer's costume, and fluffy white petticoat showed loud and daring. Her white blouse was in need of a hot iron and it was loopy-buttoned, according to Daddy.

"Hey, Sugah." Edie greeted him with a peck on the cheek.

She noticed Chet glancing at the other girls and then at her. And she noticed the stretched-out looks the other girls gave to her particular outfit. She knew without conscious thought that discussion of her clothes would spread through the little town like bind weed creeps through a summer vegetable garden.

"Honey, Grace Kelly I ain't." Edie tossed her bushy hair, threaded her arm through Chet's and tilted her chin upwards as they walked into the moviehouse.

They watched *Shane*, a western about a gunslinger who shows up at a Wyoming ranch owned by the Starret's. Joey, their young boy, is fascinated by the gun and the man behind it. Shane is taunted by the macho bad guys and tries to do the moral thing by resisting but fights ensue. At the end of the movie, Shane is wounded and bloody but sits up in his saddle and rides out of town, past the cemetery and into the sunrise.

"Of course he didn't die," Edie insisted as they left the theatre. "He just knew when it was time to skedaddle out of there."

"But it broke young Joey's heart," Chet said.

"Yeah, well, sometimes that's the way of the world. I reckon he'll survive. Kids always do." She took Chet's hand and their arms swung back and forth as they walked to Kate's.

I've heard that two weeks later at the Elks Club dance, Chet watched Lizzy Edrington twisting a single strand of cream-colored beads.

Lizzy was the town beauty, high school homecoming queen five years ago and she carried herself regally. Edie noticed Chet's eyes on Lizzy.

"She's just puttin' on the dog," Edie's voice was like a shot. "I wouldn't give her air if she was in a jug. Besides, those pearls look like a noose to me." The skin between Chet's eyes caved in to form a question mark as he turned his head and looked at Edie.

Instead of any traditional necklace, a fishhook dangled from a chain around Edie's neck. Eight years ago, GIs had come home at the end of World War II wearing dog tags on thick chains; Edie had chosen one like that. She had blunted the sharp point of a good-size fishhook by cramping it down with needle-nose pliers and filing down the barb. She had made a loop by threading thin wire through the slot at the flat end of the hook and twisted the wire to form a bail. The chain ran through the bail and snapped together. The long chain fit easily over her head and allowed the fishhook to dangle just between her breasts where it seemed to attract all eyes.

The following Friday night, they stopped at Kate's Café before going to the dance at the Grange. Martha Merrill had been in Chet's graduating class and she was standing just inside the door. Martha was married to Franklin White, the mayor, and she cast a quick, mouth-turned-down-at-the-corners glance to Edie's tackle on a chain. Chet took a step toward Edie and slightly turned his back toward Martha, as if he intended a sensitive shield for Edie – and maybe for himself, too.

But Edie tossed her head to one side like throwing open a car door, looked right at Martha and said, "Yeah, it's a size three. Big one, huh?"

Martha's hard glare moved to Chet and she gave a tiny

nod, a chilly acknowledgement of him. Then she turned and walked to the back of the little eatery. Chet knew, just knew that Martha's description would be town gossip fodder for all of next week.

Later, Chet told Edie that he'd felt prickly about the incident and she said, "Oh, I believe in catch and release. You don't have to worry about being snagged, sweetie. I'll just do the *Shane* thing one day." She hugged his arm close to her chest, squeezed her eyes small and shiny and gave Chet her tilted grin.

Sometimes, out of the blue, Edie mangled bits of popular song lyrics like Rosemary Clooney's "Come on to My House." She'd sing, "Com'ona my house, I'm gonna give you everything ... for awhile."

She would sing Perry Como's latest hit and say "... I smell peaches but the trees are bare" in place of the real words. Occasionally, her conversation seemed odd, disjointed with words mis-directed, like spark plugs pulled out of the functioning cylinder head and then randomly plugged into some strange current. Chet noticed it, ignored it or explained it to himself, to his own satisfaction. Edie's vibrancy bubbled up like sunrise even if it did sometimes seem a little less due-east.

With its bantam size population and far-flung location, MacKremmon in those days was every bit a small town. Chet had grown up there and was sensitive to each voice inflection and nuance, every tiny gesture, each eye roll, every raised eyebrow. Edie often said Chet had enough self-consciousness for both of them so she was glad she lacked it. She was never embarrassed.

Edie chatted on and on and it was a short conversational trip to talk Chet into doing things he'd never done, never even thought to do. Several times, to his own surprise, he'd found himself taking her to bars, forlorn places he'd never have gone to on his own never mind take a date to; tiny taverns far up off the highway, out of view of the tourists from Denver or Boulder or Evergreen, bars where the sad silence of solitary drinkers was broken only by the screech of their chairs against the dusty wooden floor; bars with water-mark rings on the table, the sloppy scars of beer-drinking customers.

Edie's easy laugh lit up the insides of the dank, squat little boxes like the neon signs lit up their shabby facades. She would sit face-forward with both forearms on the damp bar and then turn her head to the side as she held up her cigarette for Chet to light.

Chet's look bored through the wispy grey-white smoke right into her crinkled eyes. He knew going to dumpy bars amused her. He knew his cheeks reddened as he grinned and told his friends at the garage she was the most excitement and fun he'd ever had. He knew she was different and he knew, after only a few months, that he was in love.

The clear jet-black New Year's Eve sky was the perfect backdrop for a romance-story moon and lots of stars. The couple had rung in the new with some of Chet's friends from the garage and their laughter was bubbled in breath rime as they ran, huddled inside their coats against the cold, to the car. They were both tipsy and their shivering turned into settled, cozy warmth during the twenty mile trip. Chet pulled the Chevy up in front of the ranch, dark except for a lamp in Edie's window at the far end of the bunkhouse. He put the car in neutral and set the handbrake. He left the engine running so the little heater, mounted up under the dashboard, could continue to warm them.

The winter moon was puffed up silver-white, shiny as the bottom of a new tin can. The Mills Brothers' voices on the radio were singing. "Light the path below, above and lead us on to love," came the refrain. Chet kissed Edie and she unbuckled the belt on his dressiest jeans.

"Ah, Edie, I ah, don't think we …" Chet stammered.

"Oh, lighten up and have some fun, sweetie. It's New Year's Eve and you can't live your life in a saint's sock drawer. Who of your judgmental friends is gonna know?"

It's MacKremmon, Chet thought uselessly. *Everybody*.

They made love on the front seat of Chet's 1949 Chevrolet coupe.

"Your eyes are as dark as loamy soil, Chet, and they don't hurt you a nickel's worth. You've got that Gregory Peck thing going on with the widow's peak and you're not un-handsome," she told him, "but I think you're inexperienced." Edie put her hands, with their rough skin and bright red fingernails, around his cheeks. "It's kinda sweet. You just need more practice. Aren't you lucky you found me?" Edie buttoned her blouse and caught Chet with her sideways grin.

He got out and buckled his belt as he walked around to open the car door for her.

"See you next weekend," she'd told him. As she sashayed toward the bunkhouse, she turned and blew him a kiss. The white air puffed up in bunches before bits whisked off into the dark.

Because most of the ranch hands took themselves and their money to town on Saturday and Sunday, Edie had that time off. Marla, the rancher's wife, cooked for her husband and the few who stayed. Edie always managed to get a ride to MacKremmon and she and Chet spent every weekend together. They never went to the ranch and once Chet asked why.

"With that many men around, the place always looks and smells like a pig sty. Besides, my space is tiny and can you imagine that I have any real privacy?" she replied. "So I come over here for the weekend. Hey, aren't you glad to see me, darlin'?"

Of course he was glad to see her; so glad that some weekends, they only left Chet's tiny apartment to eat dinner at Kate's or La Cocinita, seven miles away on the highway to Fraser.

Once, as they lay in bed talking, Edie took a puff on her cigarette and said, "Lots of us girls in the South get married while we're still young'uns. But that's ancient history. You don't care what happened to me before we met, do you, Chet?"

Chet shook his head *no* and Edie snuffed out the cigarette. She giggled as he pulled the sheet up over their heads.

Chapter Two

THEIR STORY, OUR STORY, the story continues that in early September 1954, Edie lit her morning cigarette and wound her cold hands around the sluggish china mug and inhaled the deep, rich coffee aroma. She felt her throat go tart, her stomach wrench tight and she ran to the toilet to throw up. When she knelt in front of the porcelain bowl vomiting for the second morning in a row, she sighed back on her heels and rolled her eyes skyward.

"Good god," she swore aloud and clenched her jaw tight. She hated the sour grip, hated the saliva running into her mouth before the vomiting began, hated the taste of rotten oranges that came up the back of her throat – she knew what it meant and she hated it, had every time. When the clammy shakiness eased, she got up and cupped her hand under cold water from the sink faucet. She rinsed her mouth and splashed her face; she knew she had to think what to do.

Life on the Beckwith Ranch was cyclical and now the products of the spring calving were being branded and castrated. Extra cowpokes had come from nearby ranches, arriving in rusty pick-ups, more dust than metal, to help out.

Edie was cooking meals for all of them.

Shitty timing all the way around, she thought to herself.

The ranch hands would know a doctor, a place in some little town, where she could get rid of it; some of them would have been through this, of course they would. But when they crowded noisily in for breakfast, she looked at their grimy calloused hands, the thick leather gloves stiff from the blood and drool of cattle and the rusty branding irons they used on the calves and she knew she wouldn't ask.

The hands worked seven days a week for two weeks, and each morning Edie ran out of the kitchen as soon as the bacon hit the hot skillet and released its salty aroma into the breezeless air. She added ginger ale and saltines to the shopping list and Marla, who had to go into town for groceries twice a week, brought them back. Her left eyebrow rose as she handed the brown paper sack to Edie. Edie took the sack, tightened her jaw and turned away.

The work was completed and the raucous laughter about "Rocky Mountain oysters" died down. The Beckwith hands would go on to the O'Shea farm to help and Edie finally had four days off. On Saturday morning about 8 a.m., Burley Beckwith dropped her off at the garage in MacKremmon on his way to the feed store in Fraser. She got out of the pick-up, and slammed the door so hard that all four smoothing black tires vibrated. Chet was stacking cans of motor oil.

"I'm pregnant." Hands on hips, chin jutted forward, Edie blurted out the news.

The can fell out of Chet's hands, hit with the concrete floor with a *thunkt*. The smell of oil was suddenly everywhere. Edie wrinkled her nose at the odor and told him about the morning sickness and the dizziness. There was no tinge of tenderness, no romantic aura in the words. For a full minute, he didn't speak, just held his empty hands still and stared at her.

"Oh, for god's sake, say something. I'm heavin' up every damn morning and all you can do is make harvest-moon eyes at me. I don't know if this is what I have in mind for my life." Her jeans were starting to feel tight and she needed to pee.

"Uh, that's wonderful," Chet stammered.

"Oh, hush up your mouth, Chet. It is not. Neither one of us ever said we wanted a kid."

"No, it's great, it's fine. And we are getting married, Edie," Chet swallowed hard.

"What? No, I don't wanna get married. Do you know what marriage is like? It's snot-nose kids and peeling potatoes. I don't want that. I want to go on having fun."

"Look, we may not have intended for this to happen but we are going to be parents and we are getting married like normal people. There's enough talk about us as it is," Chet said. Worry pulled the skin tight around his mouth and for a second, he wasn't sure he could draw in a breath. But he took both her hands in his. He tried to pull her to him but she stood stiff and firm.

"The neighbors are gonna think what they're gonna think. People in small towns don't have nothin' else to do but talk about each other. I couldn't give a Union brass button what they think." The words snapped out of her mouth, like rivets into cowhide.

"Look, you may not care what they think but I've grown up in this town. I know what people will say, the way they'll look at him, and how they'll treat a kid whose parents aren't married." Chet felt his senses returning, logical thought settled in. "You know it and you know he'll learn the word *bastard*, too. You know what I'm saying is right. Is that what you want for our child?"

Edie looked past Chet's shoulder at a car up on the rack. The shiny center pole lifted the vehicle so a man could walk under it, look up into the guts and take a wrench to the internal parts.

"I could find a doctor."

"No." Chet pulled her close and put his arms around her. Her neck limbered and her head sagged onto his shoulder. Chet felt himself exhale, felt the warmth of realization rushing through his veins. "You couldn't. You won't."

Yep, that was me - the child they hadn't planned on. I guess every baby is conceived the same way but this is me – the story of how I began. They both always recalled that they leaned into each other and stood that way – warm and melted like grilled cheese - for a few seconds. Then she pushed him away and ran to the restroom.

Burley and Marla Beckwith congratulated them with relieved laughter and smiles, especially when Edie revealed that the father was Chet and not one of the ranch hands.
"We'll miss you," Burley told her. "But I guess that's what I get for hirin' a fiery gal. Your southern biscuits are a real hit with these cowpunchers."

"Don't you have a girlfriend who's looking for a job?" Marla quizzed her. "I don't mind handling the books but cookin' three meals a day for hungry men is not my idea of a good time." On Edie's last day, Marla presented a store-bought cake from Triumph Bakery in Grand Lake. The hands were back from the O'Shea ranch and the cake was a rare treat. The men didn't use forks or napkins – just licked their thick, rough fingers and grinned as they shoved chunks of it into their mouths, especially the frosting that spelled out "Good Luck."

After the eleven o'clock service on October 24th, Rev. Charley Lewis stood at the door and shook hands with his parishioners as they left the Fraser Baptist Church. Then he went back inside where Chet and Edie were sitting in the front pew. As Pastor Lewis came up the aisle, they stood up and walked to the altar to meet him. Four pots of yellow chrysanthemums sat spread out on a spotless white altar cloth. Pastor Lewis' wife

Belinda, in a sensible brown dress, low heels and a little brown hat, finished stacking hymnals and stood next to Edie. She clasped her hands in front of her, her eyes widened and she gave Edie a gooey, practiced smile.

The ceremony was directly out of the Baptist hymnal. In four and a half minutes, Chet and Edie were declared "man and wife." Chet kissed Edie on the cheek and Pastor Lewis congratulated them. Belinda gave each of them a tentative hug that ended with a pat-pat-pat on the back; they were official – they were on their way to being my parents.

Now that they were married, the roundness of Edie's abdomen made Chet think of the planet earth and how they were on it for the ride. Pride was edging itself into his voice and Chet beamed at the minister.

"Might be needin' you to do a baptism pretty soon, Reverend," Chet told him. Edie turned her head to look through the stained glass window at some distracting distant peak.
The couple used Chet's savings and put a down payment on a bungalow at 2012 East Street, a small frame house that teetered on the fading edge of town. Edie had stuffed her clothes into pillowcases and she flung them into the back of Chet's spotless Chevy. She settled herself in the front seat with a huge sigh. Morning sickness was past now and she grinned and puffed on a cigarette as they pulled away from Beckwith Ranch. Daddy said he remembers staring at the road ahead.

Just about emptying out his rented apartment, Chet moved a double bed and a couch into the cottage. Edie found a rocking chair at Goodwill in Winter Park and they bought a white Coldspot refrigerator, shiny as a promise, from the Sears catalogue. Together, they picked out a crib, brought it home and shoe-horned it into the second bedroom. Edie's labor was short and at 5 p.m. on March 15, 1955, at old Doc Hedstrum's office, I, Kenneth Dawson Evans, was born.

"Ken's a good name, don't you think?" Edie asked as

she rocked my seven and a half pound, dark-haired newborn self. "I had an Uncle Kenneth who moved to Atlanta. In every Christmas card, he'd tell us how successful he was. I always felt right proud that he dumped our little town and changed his life and became a big-city hot shot."

Daddy said he had nodded. Any name was fine with him. He always said his amazement and delight in me, the tiny human, came as a complete surprise. He said he often felt he couldn't breathe when he looked at me, how the awe of being a partner to creating a new tiny life seemed to remove his senses. Now he was a father, a parent – I made him that. At his own insistence, he often got up with me for nighttime feedings. Being a dad was a new sensation and the soft, powdery smell of my tiny fuzzy head, the grip of small, strong fingers, the *eep, eep, eep* sound of me gulping the bottle – all of it tapped into his sense of wonder and made him think of mortality and immortality. He called me Baby Kenny and wished his own father could have seen this child, his grandson.

And Chet's character, part of his own identity, the part he got from his father, would now, as a part of the intertwining vine of heredity, be shaping tendrils in me, his son, be the basis for it all. Parenthood created awe in Chet he hadn't known he was capable of and made him forget to care what people might think of a couple who had a baby less than five months into their marriage.

But in Edie, who was now my mother, the pregnancy and birth evidently had triggered some kind of dormant condition; aggravated a storm, seeded a cloud of doubt until it coursed into episodes of hard-raining paranoia. Giving birth seemed to bring forth jealousy, irritability and rages against gauzy injustices; rages that Chet had not known were in her.
When she was in a good mood, the world was a sunny, wonderful place filled with laughter and song.

"*Get out the way, Ol' Dan Tucker. You're too late to come to supper,*" Edie would rock me and sing songs from her Southern youth. "*Combed his hair with a wagon wheel, died with a toothache in his heel.*"

But sometimes, a sunny day seemed like a thin scrim – fleeting, ethereal and spider-like shadows seeped through the fabric and around the edges of the lightly woven day until the bright was overtaken and hard brown clots formed. When the eruptions came, dark knotted moods unleashed with speed and fury. Often hot, ugly accusations spewed like lava.

"You know I've been cooped up all day with this squalling baby and you've been out having a good time with your friends at work. I bet you were all talking about how fat I look since the baby. And you and them boys stopped for a beer on the way home, didn't you? At Hennessey's where that triflin' Swinson girl works as barmaid, ain't that right? And you think dinner should be on the table when you get home. Well, I can't build my life around a piece of meat. Here, take him, I'm going out."

She would shove me into Daddy's arms. As the wobbly screen door slammed behind her, flakes of dull-white paint jumped off the doorframe. Mama usually came walking back home within a few hours. But sometimes she might be gone for two or three days and Daddy would have to rely on Mrs. Fullenweider down the road to help out. He never knew which Edie he would find when he got home.

"Maybe we could get your mother to fly out from Georgia to stay a few weeks and help us out," Daddy offered one calm evening. He knew little about her family, but everyone had a mother.

"I done told you my mother died in jail." Daddy always said the words came out of Mama's mouth like each was encased in ice. "She was no a'count and she spent most days knee-walkin' drunk. If she wasn't stealin' money to buy liquor, she was swillin' moonshine from my granddaddy's still. I don't want to see her ever again as long as I live. And if I'd wanted to be tied down with shit and string beans, I could've stayed in Georgia with those brats."

Daddy cradled me in his arms as if he could protect me from the sound of dishes shattering against the linoleum kitchen floor.

Chapter Three

By the time I was a toddler, Mama's moods could change as rapidly as the Colorado weather. On a worthy day, she would take crosshatched peanut butter cookies out of the oven, pour cold milk into a clean jelly jar and carry the treat to the front stoop. From there, she and I could soundlessly sit and watch, in the pines and aspen and redbud just across the road, beige velveteen deer rubbing against the brown-grey scratchy bark of cottonwood trees. Short tails on the mule deer twitched and their fleece-like heads bobbled up to look at the humans and then down to nibble any edible growth. From our low flat seat, we would frequently see grouse, often a red fox and once a mountain lion, all against the backdrop of Sheep Mountain.

From the very first, I loved the wild and even as a little boy, I spent hours walking in the woods where the trees met overhead and formed a hushed, almost church-like atmosphere. The spongy ground beneath absorbed the sound of my footsteps.

"It's like you were baptized twice," Mama told me one afternoon when my four year-old self had come home with briar scratches on my hands and wild raspberries in my jeans pockets, "once by the parson in the church and once by nature in the woods. You've got the scent of the wild on you. I expect you'll always have it."

Her Southern upbringing was as prevalent in Mama's life as snowfall in the Rockies. "Southern gentlemen have good manners." She would spend hours teaching me how to shake hands. "Look the other person right in the eye. Put out your hand. Give a good, firm handshake, no limp-fish grip for you." And she taught me to say, "Yes, ma'am" and "Yes, sir."

As I got older, Mama told me stories she remembered from her own childhood in the South, Uncle Remus stories or some of the Jack Tales.

"Once there was boy named Jack and one time, Jack and his brothers were lyin' around home, doin' no good, so his daddy decided he'd set him to work. He had him a tract of land out in the wilderness of a place back up on the mountain and he set Jack to workin' on it." Mama would spin the yarn out and it almost always ended with Jack finding a wife who could bake delicious biscuits, which made both of them happy in their life together.

One late summer day, I got lost in the woods. Nothing looked familiar and I stumbled around for what seemed like a long time. When I finally saw a familiar path and found my way home, I expect my face held that look of exhausted release that almost always follows panic. Bits of branches and leaves crowded my hair and stuck to my clothes. Mama took one look at burrs on my shirt and skinned knuckles on my hands and said, "Dr. Livingstone, I presume."

I didn't know who Dr. Livingstone was but Mama's greeting included a hug and I remember that I sighed and leaned my whole body against her. The tense muscles in my neck relaxed and my higher-than-little-boy-normal blood pressure lowered. Years later, when I got to the seventh grade, I looked up Dr. Livingstone in the school encyclopedia. Being compared to an explorer made me smile.

Mama taught me to stand and sing, "Oh, I wish I was in the land of cotton, old times there are not forgotten, look away, look away, look away, Dixieland." I often chewed the inside of my cheek as I worked to remember all the words right – I had to get it exactly right. Some days, Mama sat at the kitchen table snapping beans for dinner, singing Hoagy Carmichael's "Georgia, Georgia, the whole day through …"

Mama kept peeled, sliced peaches in the freezer so she could make cobbler year-round. It was my favorite dessert and I knew she'd had a good day if peach cobbler showed up on the dinner table.

One July afternoon, we were peeling peaches for cobbler when Mama said to me, "You don't know how lucky you are, Ken, to always have perfect peaches. When I was a girl, my dad grew peaches and sold'em at our family's stand by the side of the road. He sold the perfect ones and I was 13 before I knew I could pick out a peach that didn't have a bruise or bad spot on it." Her voice was low and the words came out slowly as if as if she were struggling to decide with each word whether or not to tell me this.

"Were those Palisades peaches, Mama?" I was about five and I knew all about Colorado peaches.

"Oh, no, honey. I'm from Georgia which is a long way from here. The peaches I had when I was a girl were *Georgia peaches*." At those two words, she raised one eyebrow and nodded knowingly toward me. "Peanuts are a big crop but Georgia's not called the Peach State for nothin'."

"Is Georgia just like MacKremmon?"

"No, son," Mama said with a little energy in her voice. "Georgia is flat and dusty. Peach farms are big and take up lots of space. Sometimes the orchards go on for as far as the eye can see. MacKremmon is a tiny little speck by comparison."

"Why's it dusty?"

"Well, some summers, there's not much rain and the red

clay gets dry and dust kicks up. Farmers worry their crops won't make. If the crops don't come in, farmers don't have anything to sell for money." She used a wear-dulled steak knife to peel the peaches and it rested in her lap, on the calico print of her apron. "Some days we had potted meat on saltine crackers for lunch. My mama made our dresses out of feed sacks so we always had clothes. But I remember one fall, my sisters and I put newspaper in the bottom of our school shoes because my daddy didn't make much money farming peaches and we had to wear what we had, holes and all."

"Will I get to see Georgia?"

"As we say in the South, 'You cain't never tell.'" Mama's smile was gentle as air after a thunderstorm. "But I don't think so, Sweet Pea. It would take days to drive there. It's real hot and the air is sticky. In the summer, there are lots of mosquitoes." She put down the peach she was peeling and wiped her hands on a flour-sack dishtowel. "Sometimes, I think about things I need to see again."

The smooth-mood landscape never lasted long and the jagged-edged tempers smoldered just below the surface. Daddy got to where he could almost sense when the moods were coming, and he would take me with him to work at the garage. He always said I could amuse myself for hours with nuts, bolts and discarded car parts. Frayed cables and belts, useless dashboard dials, and knobs from broken window cranks fascinated me when I was a little boy. I learned to count with greasy spark plugs, and Daddy taught me the alphabet by saying "A is for axle, B is for brakes and C is for car." Residents who stopped by the station for gasoline or repair work noticed and word *tsk-tsk*-ed its way through MacKremmon when I was at the garage.

When he had weekends off from the garage, Daddy took me camping. "The boys are off," he'd say. He'd grab up our sparse equipment and we'd both kiss Mama good-bye. We often pitched a tent near Grand Lake, Colorado's largest natural lake, which was formed by glacial action leaving ridges of clay and rocks call moraines, Daddy loved to explain. There, I played at Lemon Beach and made sand castles with a tuna can and an old spoon. Together, Daddy and I tramped through the surrounding woods of tall pine and clattering aspen together. We often spotted red fox and once we saw a vixen with two little kits. I liked how she watched every move the skittish babies made and nudged them if they got more than a few steps away from her.

Often on long walks, I'd look at the trees and sniff the woods and listen to Daddy talk about how his father had worked on the crew that, in the late 1930s, had dug a deep and large underground tunnel thirteen miles long, with a concrete liner in diameter over nine feet.

At its deepest, the underground tunnel is 3,800 feet below the surface of the mountains. It runs in a straight line under the Continental Divide and within four miles of Rocky Mountain National Park and annually diverts approximately 260,000 acre feet of water from the Colorado River and Grand Lake, to provide irrigation for farmland and to generate electricity for five power plants.

Work on the actual tunnel had begun in 1940 but was suspended during World War II and resumed in August 1943. When the tunnel was holed through on March 31, 1944, NBC Radio broadcast the event throughout the entire United States and all the digging crewmen were heroes. U.S. Senator Alva B. Adams was the chief advocate and the tunnel was posthumously named for him.

"The whole project covered about 250 miles in the state. My dad worked on the part from Lake Granby and the work was back-breaking," Daddy told me. "All the diggers came out dusty, turning off their headlamps and coughing at the end of every day. My dad loved being outdoors so being in the dark all day really got him down. He told us many times how depressing it was. He seemed okay on the weekends and he'd take my cousin Calvin and me fishing and hiking. But he dreaded Monday morning, knowing he'd have to take his shovel and go back down into the tunnel. Eleven communities get water from the project so he felt like he was doing important work.

"Besides, he had to support his family and it was a regular paycheck from the government. So he did it. He loved us that much. Our family is Welsh, Ken, and in Wales, our ancestors worked in the mines. But that just wasn't in my dad and I don't think he ever really got used to it." We were standing in shallow water looking for trout. Daddy looked back down at the reel in his hands and sighed. "I guess the dust in his lungs is what took him."

"Am I Welsh, Dad?"

"Yes, you are but you and I are a lot taller than most Welshmen. They'd think we are giants!"

"Did all the Welshmen work in the mines?"

"Lots of them did. And they loved to sing. The opera house in Central City outside of Denver was built because the Welsh and Cornish miners wanted a place to sing. We'll drive over there and see it one day." He ruffled my hair and we went right back to quietly gazing into the champagne colored water. We were men and we knew how to fish.

Occasionally, we would drive to Lake Granby where Daddy would rent a boat from Norton Marina to take us to the middle of the lake where water the color of night reflected the blood-purple mountains. No matter what time of year it was, a scatter rug of white snow sat atop high points of the deep green peaks.

Usually Daddy pitched a tent and we camped, but one night the weather suddenly turned bitterly cold. When the unanticipated September sleet began, we checked into the Best Vu Motel near Dillie Docks. I was not yet six years old but I remember lying wide-eyed in the dark, next to Daddy in the double bed, and pulling the chenille bedspread with the blue and white bumps up over us. Daddy fell asleep but I lay there, knowing he was next to me, his warmth like an invisible blanket of security for me, his light snoring a sort of soundtrack for this new adventure. I was barely able to sleep because of the excitement of my first night in a motel. The memory of how even and soft that bed felt, how the pillow seemed huge under my boy-sized head and how even the dark seemed deeper has stayed with me, indelible in my senses. Even in my adult years, the redolent, scented fragrance of pine resin and the gentle *hlap-hlap-hlap* of the water comes back to me, real, honest and unbidden, any night I spend in any hotel and I always dream that Daddy is there, next to me, and I feel safe.

In the spring, tiny but hardy flowers like forget-me-nots and Mexican hat and Alpine avens sprang up on the forest's floor, trilling their own birth announcement. Indian paintbrush looked like I could dip them in water and watch their colors run as they swished in the breeze, next to non-moving bowls of cactus blooms. Daddy often told me, "Looking at wildflowers is not a drive-by sport. You gotta get up close and take a deep look at'em. In some ways, I guess we're all wildflowers, Ken. We're a species that occurs naturally in the place where we are found. Our roots go deep in the land."

Before I was seven, I knew that the combined petals of a flower are called the corolla and I could identify the sepal, the pistil and stamen. I knew which plants were annuals, and which were perennials and biennials. For my seventh birthday, my parents gave me a book of blank pages bound in dark brown leather – I know now that it was expensive and they must have saved up for it. They wanted me to record what I saw, write down the names of each plant and flower. I kept it faithfully, dating each entry, and inked sketches of plants and flowers, boats, mountains and animals soaked into the pages.

In the hot summer, fly fishermen posed like skyscrapers,

upright and interspersed every thirty or forty feet according to their unwritten etiquette rules, staying out of each other's range. They stood in thick rubber waders, in the flat landscape of water. There was very little talk among them as they pulled trout, rainbow and brown, out of the water. The silver sparkle of the opaque filament lines from their Redington fly rods and reels, flailing in horizontal arcs through the air, played a silent symphonic hum in my mind.

The seven-mile Yampa River begins at Flat Tops and flows into the Green River, near Echo Park in Moffett County. The local lore was that the Yampa held 1,200 fish per mile. I thought that could be true because some days, I just dropped a hook in and took out a good –sized fish. Both Daddy and I loved the way the Yampa looked calm but felt wild and appealing, the smell of the water, the way red dogwood and golden willows cast shadows that played on the tawny colored water. In the silence that enveloped us, I often thought the river must end at the just the spot I could see on the horizon because that much glistening splendor could not possibly go on for any distance; it had to come to an end somewhere. Even the scent had to stop somewhere, I thought.

When the heart-shaped aspen leaves turned yellow and clattered in the breezes, I knew fall was edging summer out of the way. After the leaves drizzled down from the trees, aspen trunks displayed brown markings that made them look like totem poles or voodoo spirit wands. They stood, arrogant and magical as a maudit tree, among the evergreens – droopy yews, holiday-like firs and majestic pines – that gave hope for the next standard of new, of predictable seasonal renewal.

Wintertime followed and I loved the often-brittle cold and piles of sparkling white that it brought. My solitary stomps in backwoods isolation often involved breaking new snow; I knew I was the first human to touch it and I felt a sense of honor, reverence and responsibility to treat it with respect. At home, I knew how to tune in the radio weather report for news about the snow around Steamboat Springs. I listened faithfully because the melting snow would become the runoff that energized the springtime river.

Chapter Four

Reggie was born eight weeks after my sixth birthday; Reggie, who had blonde hair and blue eyes and didn't really look like Dad or me. I had been a long, skinny baby and Mama had said my legs looked like strings with a knot in the middle. But Reggie was born short and pudgy with chubby hands, round thighs and fatty calves. By the time he was a year old, Reggie looked like he had been dropped into the little family. He had tight curls and ears that only seemed to fit his head as he grew into being a toddler. His blue eyes had the spark-plug glint of mischief and he was happy-go-lucky no matter what colors the day wore.

Even though I went to Ethel W. Martin Elementary School every day, I spent enough time at home to sense the rough, uneven atmosphere. It seemed to me the new baby had not brought any kind of consistent happiness with him when he arrived. Many afternoons, I gave Mama's mood a wide berth by pushing a rickety, secondhand baby carriage up and down the rutted gravel road in front of our little house. Bits of shaggy dark blue canvas had worn themselves away from the buggy's chrome frame and flapped solitary and lonely into the afternoon breeze.

As I pushed, I sang "Dixie" and other songs I knew to my baby brother. I pointed out white-tailed rabbits and big black crows.

As a toddler, Reggie dug into everything with high energy and he seemed to know no fear. Once, when he was two and a half, he grabbed the tabby kitten, Tooley, by her tail and swung her around his head yelling, "Yee-haw!" Even when the skittish young cat clawed her way back to solid earth, Reggie, who wore bandages for six days while the deep scratches healed, just laughed it off.

Reggie often watched Mama peel potatoes. She used the old steak knife with a once-shiny silver blade, now dulled to a pewter tone and chinked with use. One summer day, when Reggie was three, he grabbed the knife by its split handle and took it out to the fenced-in yard beside the house where the chickens roamed. He squinted his eyes, stuck his neck out, and threw the knife at the chickens as they scratched unaware in the dirt.

Reggie was extremely coordinated, a lot more coordinated than I was, and it irritated him that he missed the first four times. The squawking of the pursued fowl got louder and more shriek-like each time the knife flew. By the time Reggie readied himself for the fifth fling, he had identified a likely target. Dust rose in round puffy clouds and the chickens, hemmed in by big octagon-shaped holes of the chicken wire, were screeching and running in scratchy, loopy circles, noisily colliding with each other as they tried to escape.

Reggie drew back his arm and the knife left his pudgy little-child hand and hurled itself through the air, straight ahead. The blade hit her brick-red feathers, and the hen shrieked as much in surprise as in agony as she ran her gawky race around the enclosure, bright red blood mixing with the chicken yard dust. Mama went running out of the house. She held a cigarette in one hand and waved a dishtowel with the other.

"Jesus jumpin' up and down in the morning, Reggie!

Where on God's green earth did you get that knife? And what in blazes have you done, you little demon?" She screamed at the boy but Reggie stood with his hands on his hips, in a cocky conqueror-type stance as he and Mama watched the wounded hen make one more complete lap around the fenced-in space. Then the perfectly good layer fell to the ground, dead. Mama dropped her cigarette into the dust, ground it with the heel of her shoe and applied a whack to Reggie's backside.

"If there's a hell, you're on the road to it," she told him loudly. "You shake my nerves, child." I expect that a good portion of the MacKremmon population could hear her. She gritted her teeth, swatted his backside again and shoved him past me, standing at the door, and inside the house.

We had fried chicken for dinner that night. Reggie made loud, smacking noises as he ate it. Mama just rolled her eyes.

I remember when I was eight and Reggie was an into-everything toddler. We had all gone on a Sunday afternoon drive. Daddy had spent a couple of hours washing and polishing the treasured Chevrolet before he packed our family into it. We had stopped at Lake Granby and strolled around in the spongy green grass on the eastern side of the lake. Little boys we were, we were giggling, shrugging our shoulders and waving our hands over our heads so the Canadian geese that dotted the grassy areas wouldn't come near when they swooped in to eat the breadcrumbs tossed their way.

Reggie and I were dressed in our Sunday best. I wore brown pants and a carefully ironed yellow oxford cloth shirt. Reggie's little navy blue suit had short pants. Daddy was nearby, squatting on one knee, quietly laughing at our joy, watching us, handing us white ragged bits from the colorful bread bag. He had on his light tan summer Sunday suit and a wide brown tie with swirls on it. The sun made his thick, dark hair shiny.

Mama stood about ten feet away, stiff-shouldered, arms crossed in front of her, stone-like. The wind swirled the hem of her soft, sheer dress and the full, scalloped sleeves fluttered weakly. Suddenly, she turned, began to swing her arms and tilted her upper body into striding away from us. What Reggie and I called his "dad-eyes" caught the movement and Daddy snapped upright, almost falling over, as he instantaneously twisted in the direction she was going. He made a fist squeezing the bread into a tight, fuzzy ball. He crumpled the plastic bag as he glanced quickly at us.

"Don't move. Stay right here," he told us. His hands reached toward Reggie and me as if he wanted to herd us together but his eyes never really left our mother. He rushed off to catch her by the elbow and stop her harsh, forward movements. She jerked her arm away from him and leaned her pinched face toward him as she spoke. I couldn't hear what they were saying and it seemed like a long time that Reggie and I were there in the sunshine, shivering, shooing the geese away, until our parents came back to us.

Reggie was about four when he noticed Mama and Daddy sipping a whiskey on Friday evenings. For several weeks, he badgered them about it. One hot, cloudless summer evening, Mama and Daddy sat, jaws clenched against the tirades, in straight-back wooden rocking chairs on the front porch. Reggie wouldn't let up, kept hammering to taste the drink.

Finally, Daddy heaved a big sigh and slammed his hands on the flat arms of the rocker. The dry wood slats of the porch creaked as he tipped the chair forward, lifted himself up out of it and went inside the house. In just a minute, he came back holding two small Mason jars, with a splash of dark liquid sloshing in the bottom of each.

"Ok," Daddy said in that exasperated tone parents often use on little boys, "come here, both of you."

Reggie flung his arms, dropping the cat to the ground, and strode up three steps toward our father. I put down my book and stood up. I wasn't sure I wanted to but I did.

"Here," Daddy held out the glasses, "taste it."

Reggie shot a commanding look at me and I stepped forward, took the jar and looked at the liquid. I drew breath in through my nose and took a big sip of the whiskey.

"Ahhhkkkk … haaa … ahhhh." My throat burned and I grasped my neck with one hand while the other held the jar straight out, away from myself. Daddy said later that my eyebrows were three inches taller and my eyes popped wide open, showing shiny white. My tongue stuck itself out faster than a jack-in-the box.

As I was panting for air, Reggie reached forward and took the other jar. His head leaned back on his neck as he threw the fiery liquid down his throat.

"Ahhh," he said smacking his lips and righting his head, "that's pretty good." He wiped his mouth with the back of his hand, cowboy style. "Can I have some more?" He held the jar out to Daddy.

"No, you cannot have more," Chet told him sternly. Aside to Mama, I heard him say, "So much for 'give them some, that'll cure'em!'"

"No, you certainly cannot have more!" Mama frowned and agreed. "Lord have mercy, that kid's got spunk," she said quietly to Daddy.

I had had a special blanket, a blue one that had been with me since birth. I napped with it, held it in my lap while I ate and dragged it in the dirt when I played outside. At the age of three and a half, I dropped it one day and never looked back.

Reggie never showed any interest in a blanket but when he started walking, he found an old once-red sock. Mama said she never saw its mate and thought it materialized alone, unaccompanied in the world, determinedly solo. Once he spotted it, Reggie carried it with him everywhere – naps, meals, rides in the car or red wagon – everywhere.

For months, Reggie had been picking up random items

and putting them in the sock. Mama said he must be part crow because he was always attracted to shiny things. Odd nails, loose coins, paperclips, ball bearings – they all got dropped into Big Red, as Reggie called the sock. Reggie held the sock by the now-stretched cabled top and the heavy bottom toe area took on a smooth, round ball shape.

Three mornings a week, Reggie went to pre-school at the Methodist Church in MacKremmon. Mama thought that being around kids his own age was good for the energetic little boy and he was learning colors, shapes and the alphabet. On Monday, Wednesday and Friday mornings, Mama dropped Daddy off at the garage, took me to school and delivered Reggie to his busy, active class. Luanne Fullenweider was his teacher. Other kids might cry and hug a parent's leg but not Reggie. He always made a mad dash into the classroom and was boisterously involved in an activity with other kids before Mama could wave good-bye.

She hadn't noticed Big Red in Reggie's hand that morning so she was surprised when she went to pick him up at noon and Luanne motioned her to come inside. It was a teacher work day and I was home from school so I was with Mama when she parked the car. We went into the classroom to find Reggie seated at a low table, arms firmly crossed over his chest, chin held high.

"I'm so sorry to have to talk to you about this but it seems Reggie brought the red sock to school today – and this was in it." Luanne put her closed right hand on the little table and uncurled her fingers. Lying in the palm of her hand was Edie's fish hook necklace. Both women looked at the boy whose chin only increased in altitude.

"At circle time, it was Reggie's turn to say the day of the week." She looked at Reggie who pretended not to notice. "Unfortunately, Toby Wilkerson shouted it out before Reggie could say, 'Wednesday.' Reggie wasn't happy and he swung the sock. The large prong broke through the cotton. It caught Toby on the left cheekbone and well, we bandaged him up but it made a gash. We called Cynthia and she came and picked him up."

Mama's jaw firmed and her eyes narrowed and she glared at Reggie who continued to focus on numbers one through ten on the far wall.

"I'm so sorry." Mama was controlling her voice by gritting her teeth together. I could see the muscles around her eyes tighten and she turned to Luanne. "I'll call and see how he is."

Toby was the youngest of three boys. The oldest boy was Richard Clark Wilkerson, Junior, known in MacKremmon as Little Dickie. Little Dickie and I were in the same class at school and while Mama often had to nod or smile, she absolutely refused to talk to Cynthia Wilkerson. Cynthia was pleasant enough. But Mama wanted nothing to do with a parent who had produced flamboyant Little Dickie. Still, she knew she had to make the call.

"I'll let her know we are concerned."

"Of course. It was an unfortunate incident." Luanne folded her arms across her chest indicating she had done her duty, and was finished discussing the whole thing. Mama jerked Reggie by the hand and led him outside to the car. When we got home, she smacked his behind with a wooden spoon but Reggie lifted his chin and never cried.

"You need to behave yourself at school. And don't you *ever* touch my necklace again." Her index finger shook at Reggie's face. "It's mine. It means something to me and I'm the only one who touches it. Are you getting all this?"

I felt the responsibility of keeping a big-brother eye on my curly-haired sibling. Reggie seemed to effortlessly snatch attention from every possible situation and it seemed to mean very little to him. But I craved Mama's warmth and affection for myself and often purposely took on tasks that were hard, required strength and focus, just to hear her praise, to feel her acceptance and approval.

"Kenny, you caught and cleaned that fish all by yourself? It's a beautiful trout and you did a good job, son. Let's dip it in cornmeal and fry it for supper."

"You hung up the wash, Ken. I didn't know you could reach the clothesline. You're sure a big help to your ol' mama."

I was always on the lookout for little ways to make her happy; thinking ahead, anticipating her wants kept me vigilant. I felt like I could thrive for days on kind words, got through the ugly, screaming times by remembering a soft, tender look or a sweet powdery-smelling hug she had given me on a happy-hours filled day.

Sometimes, especially if she had been gone for a night or two, she'd come home and hold me in the circle of her arms while she told me bedtime stories of things I'd done as a little kid – *my stories*, I always thought, *stories where I am important. She sees me up close, I wasn't a drive-by story.*

But the dark moods clotted like heavy traffic on a foggy highway, one followed another too closely and before one had really ended, it collided with another. I sometimes thought Mama's eyes looked like a headlight – glaring, with no discernable shading or depth, just an angry glower that bore straight ahead, not fueled by any inner depth or reason.

During one of those moods, Mama was lying propped on the couch with her feet up, reading *Modern Romances* magazine, knocking flaky ashes into a heavy-bottomed glass ashtray that rested on her abdomen. She moved the ashtray to the end table and let the burning cigarette rest there. In one hand, she held a red and blue cellophane packet of Lance salted peanuts. In the other hand, a bottle of Coca-Cola. She carefully shook peanuts from the packet into the dark liquid. The little salty treats bounced around, coating themselves in the carbonated drink. Then Mama tipped the bottle up and fizzy Coke and crunchy peanuts poured into her mouth.

The gray sky of a rare fall thunderstorm made the room seem close, uncomfortably intimate as if sweaty hands were holding me. It was claustrophia-causing. Both of us boys were in the bedroom we shared and Reggie was in a deep toddler nap. Even the harsh crash of thunder and the sulfur-smelling lightning didn't wake him.

But I could not sleep and the depressing drab sky seemed to bear down on me, push my spirit deep, cause my chest to cave inward. In the pre-rain darkness, I could feel my breath catch and my heart beat faster. I had a sense of aloneness and the heavy weight of the clouds made me afraid. Loud thunder clapped and I called out.

"Mama," I heard my own shaky voice.

"Mama?"

No response. I made two fists, the tense muscles giving me strength, and used them to bunch the pillow up under my head.

"Mama." I said it louder.

The door to the room flung open and the pillow was yanked from under my left ear and it smacked down on my head, shoulders, and legs.

"How can I have any peace and quiet with you yelling? *How??*" Mama's jaw was clenched. The pillow went up and down, hard in her strong hands, and the room was full of feathers. I rolled up tight in a ball and used my palms-up hands to keep the empty cotton ticking from stinging me, again and again.

"Now, clean that up before your father gets home." She left the room and slammed the door.

I became more and more alert to my mother's moods and movements; it paid off for me to know where she was at any moment. After church services, Little Dickie and I would meander around the edges of the cemetery where ancestors from both our families were buried. Hands in pockets, I usually kicked at the dust with the toes of my Sunday shoes while we talked.

Dickie always kept his carefully shined shoes out of the dry beige dust. Frequently, he straightened the collar of his ironed oxford cloth shirt or waved his hands expressively. Dickie was colorful and in a town where the houses all looked alike and people wore what they saw others wearing, he stood out. We talked about everything.

"Your hair looks different. It's long. Did your mom let you skip a haircut?" I asked him one Sunday morning.

"Yeah, it looks great, doesn't it?" Dickie swept a hand down over the hair that covered his forehead. "It's called a mop top – you know, like the Beatles."

"What's the Beatles?"

"It's a band. Didn't you see them on the Ed Sullivan show on TV?"

"Naw, we don't have a TV. And I don't think my mama would let me have a mop top."

I had never thought much about my hair. Mama cut our hair, Reggie's and Daddy's and mine. Every five or six weeks, she put a kitchen towel around our necks, first Daddy's and then me and then Reggie, and pulled out a pair of small, thin silver shears and clipped away. She always shook out the towel in their backyard, just where it met the woods.

When I asked why, she had told me, "The birds use the hair and twigs and bits of lint to make their nests. Hair's like life, it's only ours for a short time. Besides, lots of things have another life."

While Little Dickie and I talked, we kept eye contact. But I often adjusted my head slightly or moved my body a little so I could keep Mama in the corner of my eye all the time. If she came out of church and turned toward the car, I immediately and often abruptly ended the conversation. I had to get to the car at the same time she did – her happiness and her pleasure in me was all that mattered.

"Gotta go," I'd say to Dickie as I immediately torqued

my body if she headed in the direction of the Chevy.

One Sunday, I was deep into listening to Little Dickie talk. We were nearly twelve, just at the age when we realized some forms of life existed outside our town, and Dickie was talking about getting out of MacKremmon.

"When I grow up, I'm gonna go to Hollywood and be in the movies. I hate being called '*Little Dickie*', can you imagine being called Little Dickie? I'm gonna change my name. I'll get an agent who'll find me the right scripts and I'll become a movie star." Dickie seemed to know a lot about Hollywood and the movies. "I'm gonna throw away these tacky cowboy boots and wear stylish, expensive clothes and go to wild parties."

The talk of leaving MacKremmon and being reborn in some other life was as foreign to me as flying to the moon in a hubcap. The vivid details of Dickie's descriptions crowded my mind and edged out the vigilance. Mama's hand was on the Chevy's door handle and Reggie was crawling into the back seat when she screamed my name.

"I don't want you hanging around with that kid. He's queer as a two-dollar bill." She swatted the back of my head as I got into the car.

Mama was still angry when we got home and sent me to my room. I remember thinking I wasn't sure what a queer two-dollar bill looked like, maybe the picture of George Washington had two heads. But Mama's anger, that omen of apartness, scared me. And while I still talked with Dickie, it was the last time my watchfulness failed me.

True to the pattern, several lazy summer days, maybe even a week of them, streamed calmly by. Mama sang "*Burnin' like a heat wave*" or "*Blame it on the bossa nova with its magic spell*" while she scrambled breakfast eggs or swept the kitchen floor.

But the lyric evenness was gashed late one afternoon as suppertime approached. Mama's anger had been whipped up by some unknown thought or action – some remark someone had made to her at the grocery store or a look the post office clerk had given her – who knows. She gestured wildly for me to get my schoolbooks and a couple of broken car parts off the kitchen table.

"Now, godamnit!" she screamed at me. Her right hand held a lit cigarette and as she swept the radiator cap and spiral notebook off the table, the hot ember at the tip caught me on the left wrist. The scorching heat burned through the flesh right where the wrist bends the hand from the arm, where the bone trusts thin skin to protect it. The searing contact between hot coal and unpadded flesh happened in a heartbeat. My eyes locked on the round spot, already looking like a tiny bonfire had burned and was now out, leaving an edge of crumpled skin around the sudden little blaze.

"Lord have mercy, Kenny, I'm sorry," Mama told me, "but you shouldn't leave your crap all over everything."

I stood very still, like I was waiting for a fish to bite, and held my left wrist in my right palm. I looked from the singe to Mama's face and back again. She had done this, given this to me and I wasn't sure what it meant. She put the cigarette to her lips and took a puff and exhaled before she tipped her chin down and looked at me again.

"C'mon, let's get some Watkins salve on that." She put cold water on it and patted it dry with a cotton dishtowel. Then using her ring finger, she lightly tapped unguent onto the charred skin. I twisted up my face and heavied my teeth tight together so I wouldn't cry. When Daddy got home, Mama told him they were having baked sweet potatoes, collard greens and pork chops for dinner.

"Those potatoes in the oven make the whole house smell good, don't they?" She had put on red lipstick and she ran her fingers through her hair as she greeted Daddy. Then she told him about the "little burn" on Ken's wrist and how it had been "an accident." When Daddy held the lightweight, boy-sized wrist in his own hand and asked me if I was ok, I just nodded.

During the next week, I would look at the nubby little red circle and rub it gently with my fingers, taking a kind of odd pleasure in the delicate pain, the little dose of suffering imposed on me. The spot on my wrist healed over and formed a round, shiny patch surrounded by a bumpy circle.

In the years to come, I often glanced at the cicatrized spot, used it like a mirror to show me who I was, reflect my individuality back to me; a job a mother might have done. This glossy little spot, so awful in its creation, served in some odd way, to validate me even while it brought back wistful memories.

In the years that followed, I would touch it without conscious thought in much the same way a woman, shocked, might cover her mouth with her hand.

Chapter Five

EACH OF MAMA'S CHURNING CHAOTIC MOODS was followed by an almost liquid serenity, a sweet time when hours flowed like a summertime stream and carried us languidly along. Days would pass, one into another, like red and green canoes sloping down Clear Creek without bumping into each other. My mind kept these times like shiny rocks worn smooth by centuries of water running over them. During the bad times, I often consciously retrieved one of these glistening mental geodes, held it up to the light in my mind so I could focus on it, examine it carefully and ignore the raging current swirling around me, around all of us.

I craved Mama's love, not in a conscious-thought way but in a basic, intrinsic gnawing that came from my very boy-essence. The spirit that saturated the palpable body wanted that love. Everything that lives yearns for mother-love - baby birds, puppies, whale calves, lion cubs – all hanker toward maternal intertwinedness. I was no exception.

I wanted each breath to be the simultaneous oxygen of life entering the lungs of both bodies, braiding us, interweaving our spirits so we, mother and son, would be slip-stitched together; a twining of two spirits, one new, vulnerable and craving and the other older, straight-backed and knowing. I did all I could to keep that soul-deep tangle, to hold it dear and hope it held me, hope the crosshatch of feelings bore the weight of my yearning without tearing or pulling apart.

One night she watched us brush our teeth, read us a book, tucked me and Reggie in and picked up the car keys. She walked out the front door. I heard the Chevy's ignition start and the gears grind as the car pulled out onto the empty dark road. I had gotten out of bed and walked three steps to the door of our room and I saw Daddy standing there. His arms hung limply at his sides and shoulders sagged – he looked inches shorter - as he always did when she drove off. With the slow movements of sadness, he closed and locked the front door and turned off the front porch light. I crept back to bed. I was not yet eleven and Reggie was four and a half when she left, departed, went away.

The next morning, Daddy woke us, fed us, and got us off to school. He called Mrs. Fullenweider, Luanne's mother, and arranged for Reggie to go to her house after his morning program. That was the schedule for several days and since it had happened before, we didn't think much about it.

When Mama hadn't come home by the end of the fourth day, Daddy told Del he needed to leave the garage early.

Later, when Daddy told us the story, he said Del told him, "Well, only the two people in a marriage know what's going on. And sometimes, one of them isn't sure."

Daddy said he didn't know how he was going to find the right words to tell us. But Del told him that family is what matters so he'd put down the bent windshield wiper he was holding, wiped his hands and headed home.

That evening, Daddy sat across the dinner table from us. He looked down at the fork he held between his forefinger and thumb. His shoulders drooped as he told us of the fear he'd been holding in his heart.

"I don't know that she's coming back this time." I

followed his gaze. He stared at the spoon as he laid it on the table upside down, the bowl's hollow created a curved back, emptying itself.

Reggie was feeding a scrap of pork sausage to Tooley. I was chewing my last bite of fried potatoes and I almost choked I swallowed so fast.

"What? Whadda you mean, Dad? Of course Mom's coming back. She always comes back." I heard a hollowness in my voice, a void where conviction had always been, should have been now.

As Reggie and I watched, Daddy pushed his chair back and got up from the kitchen table. He lifted the oblong silver-grey metal dish and put the butter in the refrigerator. He closed the refrigerator door and suddenly all three of us were aware of the whir of the compressor motor, a sound we normally never recognized, but now identified, and it filled the little kitchen like heavy air before a thunderstorm. Daddy's empty hands flopped to his sides and he stood staring at the blank whiteness of the appliance.

"I don't know, Ken. But I don't think we should be too hopeful." He turned to face us. "She's never been gone this long before. And I didn't want to tell you boys but – well, her clothes are gone and so is the brown suitcase."

Mama's fishhook necklace had always hung dangling, like it had thrown a chummy arm around the shoulder of the dark wood frame of the dresser's mirror. When Daddy realized the necklace was gone, he knew.

We watched as Daddy sat down in his chair, his shoulders and his head bent forward like they were searching the air near his heart for answers. Reggie was sitting with Tooley in his lap and as he stroked her, he fixed his eyes at one spot between her ears. I looked at my father and my brother and wondered why we were all silent. *Why doesn't somebody say something? How can we just sit here? Why aren't we screaming, wide-eyed and wild, tearing-our-clothes crazy with the loss?*

I looked closely at Daddy's face and saw him focusing on the chipped linoleum floor. Over the four days, I think he had figured it out – she was gone. The grieving process had begun for him. But we were hearing the truth about our abandonment for the first time.

"If Mama's got the car, who's gonna drive me to school?" Anger spurted loud in Reggie's voice, reflecting his little boy reality. Suddenly, in one fluid movement, he stood up from his chair and threw the cat to the floor. Tooley landed on her feet and, without a backward glance, ran across the dull braided rug, heading for the door. Heavy footsteps took Reggie into the room we shared and the door slammed.

I pushed my chair back, took my plate to the counter, grabbed up my jacket and marched outside and into the woods. Without looking back, I headed into comfort of the woods, the scent of the wild. Many times, I'd told her, "I'd walk across Rabbit Mountain to be with you, Mama." Now, I walked toward it alone, the goal vanished, blank, not existing anymore. I walked until deep into dark that night.

Edie, our mother, Daddy's wife, the female presence in our lives, was gone, leaving those roles empty, gaping. Quicker than a gnat can bat an eyelash, it was the news in MacKremmon – at Kate's, after church, in the grocery store aisles, across backyard fences. She had gone, said the gossips, vamoosed and left Chet and the boys.

I hurt so bad that I looked around, searched my body for a gaping hole, a bloody puncture, a nasty wound – some site of the terrible injury that brought so much pain. Why she had gone? What was so important that she left? What idea or adventure had crooked its finger, issued the siren call, lured her away? How could we - Daddy and Reggie and I - drop down in importance to her, fall to a lower rung of her ladder of attention and affection? How could I love her so much and see that love brushed off like unwanted lint, swatted away like an irritating insect? How could she give us up, Reggie and me, hand us over, let us down? How could she be not up close with us anymore?

Reggie's little-boy understanding didn't offer him much comfort and his solution was to go find her.

"Let's go," he said on Saturday morning. He grabbed one of my hands in his and pulled. "Let's go find Mama. You know she'll come back if we just go find her." Reggie planted his feet and pulled back so that his body formed a diagonal slant to the ground. Strain showed in the tense, ropy muscles of his mostly-cheeks face. I didn't know what to do so I jerked my thin hand away from my brother's chubby ones.

Reggie cried sloppily, nose and eyes twisted downward, tears running and dripping from his chin. I felt bad about it and my eyes drooped. I felt my shoulders curve with the awful, burdensome weight of inexplicably knowing, that even if we could find her, our mother was not coming back. My older brother, elder-child reasoning wouldn't let the dream, the fantasy of finding her, even race through my thoughts. Somehow, my boy-mind knew there would be no return, no joyous homecoming, no restoring or replacing what was gone, lost, missing, subtracted from our lives.

We weren't going looking for our mom, Reggie suddenly just knew it. His hands dropped to his sides. I turned away and I guess he watched my blue and brown plaid back get smaller and smaller as I headed toward the dark comfort of the woods. I glanced back to see Reggie's eyelids slowly cover his eyes and his neck sag backward and as his head dropped back, his mouth open. The sadness and grief knotted inside him and I think it came out soundlessly all the way into the years to come.

For two weeks after Mama left, my mind seemed cloudy, like frazzled grey puffs had replaced thoughts. Those clouds needed seeding so the nebulous droplets could congregate, coagulate, form themselves into words. I tried to think.

Wednesday evening was quiet. Dark was just beginning to push the sun out of its way when I sat down on the stoop, next to Daddy.

I chewed the inside of my jaw as my mind organized broken bits of language into comprehensible queries about our mother; formed actual questions from the cyclone swirls of *why*. Daddy and I were sitting feet flat on the ground, knees up, as the day folded. Reggie was playing in the straggly grass of the front yard, dangling a string in front of Tooley who batted first the black paw and then the brown one at the delicate bait.

"Daddy," I curved my back so my head sloped toward his knees where his arms rested, "why did Mama leave us? She has left us, hasn't she." It was more of a statement; there was really no question in the utterance or in my mind.

I watched as Daddy blew flimsy grey smoke upwards and ground the cigarette butt under the toe of his shoe. He put his arm around my shoulders and drew me to him while keeping his vision fixed on Rabbit Ear Range, not far distant. He was silent for a full minute.

I knew that Mama had driven off in Daddy's spotless pride-and-joy Chevy, the one he'd spent years working on, the one with the fender skirts, front sun visor and dual exhausts, the one he spent every Saturday afternoon polishing. She'd gotten into the car and headed off, into the freedom of the darkness, into whatever was out there past the small town's limits, into whatever was past the defining borders of our little family.

"I don't know where she went, son. I know she loved you and Reggie as much as she possibly could. She battled her own demons every day. I guess she had to leave us to fight them some more. I try to think that she was looking to find healing. She had to go to look for it on her own. She loved you boys."

"Was it something I did, Dad? If I'd kept a closer eye on Reggie and not let him get into trouble, do you think …" I leaned over and my cheek found the soft fatherly flannel of Daddy's old shirt.

"Ken, she loved you very much and that's the thought you want to hold in your heart. She loved both of you, never forget that. The rest of it – well, it's almost not worth thinking about."

"But what about your car? You love that Chevy."

"Maybe she'll take good care of it and maybe it'll remind her of us. Now, come and help me peel some potatoes for supper. We just have to get on with it."

After we knew Mama was really gone, I could hear Reggie struggling to choke back his tears. But my hurt was so leaden, weighted so far down, so canyon-deep inside that I couldn't cry.

Why did she go? What could I have done to make her stay? Why didn't I sense that she was unhappy, unhappy enough to leave us? Could I have fed the chickens more often or made my bed every day so she wouldn't have left? Whether the boy-aged thoughts made sense or not, they jerked their way through my mind like a fan belt with a nick in it.

Chapter Six

When I thought about Mama, my mind showed her features gauzy and vague. Her face was always clouded by wispy, grey-white smoke tendrils from the cigarette she never-endingly held. She puffed smoke that wafted upward over her fair skin and into her matted, unkempt hair, maybe the way Daddy had seen her in the seedy bars, in the early, dizzy days. I always pictured her smiling and looking softly, lovingly at me.

I never forgot my first cigarette. A clot of men and boys leaned over, their heads under the hood, and looked into the 289 cubic engine of the straight-shift 1968 Ford Mustang, the first of its kind anyone in MacKremmon had seen up close, in real life. It belonged to Daddy's cousin Cal who had bought it new off the showroom floor, the only brand-new car he'd ever owned, and had driven it from Denver to visit us, to share it, to show it off.

The car with its long hood and short deck was a sleek metallic blue. It had a pop-open gas cap, a tilted steering wheel and air conditioning that was fully integrated into the dash. The men in MacKremmon had never seen anything like it and wolf whistles and sounds of "ahhhhh" greeted its arrival and display.

They all wanted to sit in the high-back driver's seat. The

two front seats were bucket style with a console and they had three-point shoulder-lap seat belts, replacing the lap belt that had been standard until now. The speedometer numerals went from 10 to100, white against a black background. This was the High Country Special sold only in Denver.

All the males bent their heads to fit under the sky of the propped open hood and their eyes looked, green with the greed of looking jealously, down into the black engine hold. They talked and pointed and lifted dark, oily parts - admiringly, approvingly - and enjoyed the sense of being awed. Cal wiped down invisible specks and tiny smudges, anything to stay in direct contact with the prized vehicle. None of this was lost on me as I held the car in a kind of reverential, mystical view. Too young to drive, I just wanted to sit on the jet-black upholstery of the driver's seat. But the sense of the mysterious, of honoring the unattainable kept me still.

About two hours into the group inspection, Cal straightened up, leaned his hip against the front fender and shook a cigarette out of the pack. He held the boxy red and white Lucky Strike pack sideways ttoward me. I was tall and looked older than my thirteen years.

"You want one?"

I looked stupidly at it for just a second, and then my hand reached toward the package. With my index finger and thumb, I pulled the cigarette out of the cardboard container. I held it, stared at it for another second before I remembered what to do with it.

Cal clicked open a shiny silver Zippo lighter. His thumb ratcheted the flint and a flame jumped into existence. His cigarette was clamped between his lips and he held the short fire to the tip of the white circle with brown filling. His eyes almost crossed as he looked at the flare, waiting patiently until it had done its job.

Then he lifted his eyes to me, and held out his hand with

the flaming lighter toward me. I quickly and nervously put the cigarette between my lips as my eyes watched the steady little blaze meet the tip. I inhaled and coughed just a little. I wanted to cough more but the desire, the need to be grown up, competent, and able to handle the almost-alive kick of the hot tobacco won out over the urge.

Even now, over thirty years later, I often wonder if I started smoking as a way to feel connected to Mama, a wish to be like her, to be borne to her, to be intertwined on wisps of rising exhaled smoke, smoke that would find her and mingle us magically together.

Chapter Seven

THE PIKE'S PEAK GOLD RUSH OF 1858 and discovery of the valuable metal near Central City in 1859 brought explorers with brand new pick axes and shiny shovels to the wilderness called the Colorado Territory. Miners searched on the hillside and in caves for telltale outcropping of rocks and chinked off bits of stone to look for glimmers of gold. Panners squatted at the thin edge of icy mountain streams and scooped up sporadic bumps that bore flecks of sparkly pyrite, fool's gold. Complex ore was crushed into powder. Water was painstakingly poured and each tiny drop was sloshed over the *poudre* which was carefully sifted, held close to the eye and examined. Unwilling flakes were attentively picked out and only rarely did a good-size nugget show up. Mining and panning for gold and silver was precise, exhausting work that rarely paid off in a big way.

Alfred Nobel invented dynamite in 1867 and in just a few years, miners in the southwest part of the US were using it to break through large chunks of rock and look for precious metals. Many men and some women tried various approaches. Everyone believed he or she would hit the jackpot. Few did.

For several years, Grant Turner MacKremmon had spent

a few years mining for gold but found little and barely eked out enough to feed himself. Gradually, he discovered he was good at fur trapping and took enough beaver and rabbit pelts to town to keep provisions in his pack. Those basics – flour, sugar, lard, coffee – along with the meat from animals he shot kept him fed. Living alone and tending only to himself and his horse suited MacKremmon's style and the years slipped gently if not always comfortably by.

By late 1875, many miners had moved upstream along the South Platte River and the Colorado Gold Rush was underway. Having tried his hand at panning, he knew the sad frustrations of the crowded mining camps and he was glad not to be in that smelly, irritable tangle.

MacKremmon was riding in an open spot northwest of the center of the dry lonely Colorado Territory when his horse spotted a rattlesnake. His Appaloosa reared up, pawing the air with its front hooves. MacKremmon grabbed for the horse's sparse mane but missed and lost his balance in the creaky saddle. He fell to the ground and heard the bone in his lower left leg snap. The snake, rare in the cool weather of early fall, slithered away.

Once he calmed his horse, MacKremmon pitched a makeshift shelter in a flat, open space. He intended only a temporary camp and dragging his leg, the Scottish trapper managed to wedge one end of a tarp between two huge boulders and rig-tie the other end to a cottonwood tree. The slight shelter was just a few steps from a delicate stream, and after tethering the still-panting horse to the tree, MacKremmon, exhausted, drank cool water, inched his way under the canvas and lay with his head on his sweat-worn saddle. Legend says he believed he would die – starve, freeze to death, or become a pre-hibernation meal for a bear.

On the third day of his painful existence, he was in and out of consciousness in the flimsy encampment when two horses pulling a rattling buckboard wagon came along. A young doctor and his very pregnant wife had somehow either gotten separated from or purposely left a wagon train from the east. The autumn sun was being pushed down just below the deep purple mountain peaks. In the twilight, MacKremmon's puny campfire attracted the travelers' attention.

Doctor Wade Hampton Nolen and his wife Minnie Agnes were both from old South Carolina families. Dr. Nolen was young when the worst fighting of the Civil War had occurred near his home but the suffering he saw helped him make up his mind to study medicine. His parents sent him *up north* to Harvard medical school. They were not thrilled when, after graduation, he announced he was heading west.

Now, he was educated, eager and almost totally inexperienced. But he didn't let lack of practice stop him from helping the ragged, feverish MacKremmon. Using a couple of straight, stout aspen branches and muslin torn from Minnie Agnes's trousseau petticoat, the doctor set and bound the trapper's leg.

Minnie Agnes bathed MacKremmon's forehead and neck in cool water her husband had hauled from the stream. Wade fed dry wood to the fire. With a wedding-ring patchwork quilt from Minnie Agnes' hope chest around their shoulders, the doctor and his wife shared a meal of cornmeal spoon bread and hot coffee. Minnie Agnes soothed MacKremmon with her quiet Southern tones and by lifting the wooden spoon to his mouth, she got him to swallow a few bites. Wade gave him a mild sedative and Minnie Agnes tucked an old wool army blanket around him.

The next morning, according to the story, MacKremmon woke with all his senses about him for the first time in days. Out of gratitude and possibly self-interest, he asked the doctor and his wife to stay. Wade looked at Minnie Agnes. She put her hand on her round, hard, low-hanging belly and nodded. Three days later, in a dry, dusty open spot with the Colorado mountains in sight, the Nolen's child, Adam, was born. They didn't know it then but those were the first four residents of MacKremmon.

Colorado was admitted to the Union on August 1, 1876. By 1877, trapping was a memory for Grant MacKremmon and he had hammered together a wooden general store on the north banks of Muddy Creek, a tributary of the Colorado River. The creek meandered through eroded shale that gave the water a chocolate color and its name. From the creek, a man with a pole and a hook could take out plenty of fish for dinner. Plums, strawberries and even rhubarb grew wild on the river's bank. Existence might have been basic but with food and water accessible, it was possible.

When the snow melted in the mountains, spring runoff flowed through the two narrow streets of the newborn town, turning them into grubby ruts. Horses, wagons and pedestrians – some town residents, some just folks passing through - got stuck in the dark goop and had to be pulled out. Strangers, townspeople, everyone pitched in to help – there was lots of yelling, laughing, cursing, slipping and sliding and then everyone went to the saloon for a drink. Friendships were made. Local business thrived. Within a few years, mines were tapped out and trappers and adventure-seekers decided to stop their wandering and put down roots.

Thomas Colwell Gregory and his sister Ernestine stopped in MacKremmon for a bath and a hot meal. They were headed to Utah where Thomas hoped to work on the Transcontinental Railroad; the Chicago Burlington Quincy was scheduled to reach Denver by 1882 so plenty of jobs were available.

Ernestine was 22 years old and had taught school for five years in their native Tennessee. She took off her bonnet and shook trail dust out of her red hair as Thomas tethered their horses to the hitching post in front of the boarding house. It was noon and Grant MacKremmon was standing on the wooden sidewalk, about to enter the saloon for lunch. He noticed her immediately. He was twelve years her senior. They were married one month later. Grant and Ernestine had six children and were married for forty-three years.

Soon the streets were widened and scraped and traffic increased. The town's general store served as the social center where gossip was exchanged and news passed on with the purchases and barters. A noisy brothel opened its doors. The saloon hosted a Sunday morning church group, the piano going from plinkey honkey-tonk to deep-toned hymns overnight. But the town's drawing card was something that similar towns lacked - a real medical doctor.

In 1879, Horace Tabor's Matchless Mine in Leadville began to produce silver, what would turn out to be $7.5 million of it. Just twenty-two miles from there, a town of 1.3 square miles became widely known as MacKremmon even though the name was not officially recognized until 1895. Located 97 miles from Denver, the town is set where the headwaters of the Colorado River meet Blue River and Muddy Creek - the right location for a community. Miners had traded in their shallow pans for raw lumber and hammers; trappers had become shopkeepers, butchers or ministers. Whether they brought their families or formed them after they arrived, many found the community welcoming and the settlement grew.

Ernestine led the campaign to build a proper school and recruit teachers. Gradually, residents added a couple of churches, enlarged the general store, and paved the roads. In 1899, the US Postal Service recognized MacKremmon as a mailing address, proof that the town of 396 was officially established.

During World War II, MacKremmon hosted a US POW camp for German captives. The prisoners were friendly with the locals and were probably so grateful to be out of the fighting that none ever tried to escape. There was no patrolled fortification and during the day, the men left camp to work in the wood mills and harvest ice so local iceboxes stayed full. The prisoners even formed a little orchestra with instruments donated by the locals, and they would sit behind the wobbly-post fencing, playing concerts and entertaining the town folk.

Daddy had often told us boys about watching the well-fed, grinning prisoners line up and march single file to the makeshift movie theatre, set up in the town square. They would laugh at the movie playing out on an old bedsheet, make comments in German while punching each other's arms or slapping each other on the back. Afterwards, they marched happily, noisily back to the camp. One of the prisoners had given Daddy a toy biplane he made out of two military ration cans and Daddy frequently showed it to us boys. The town missed the hum of activity and air of joviality when, at the end of the war, the prisoners were all sent to southern US states for retraining.

Years later, when the highway from Denver cut its path to the big-name ski cities, the closest exit ramp was six miles from MacKremmon. A gas station and two fast food joints inflated almost immediately between the ramps. Huge signs directing travelers went up on the highway. Vans and SUVs could get off the interstate, fill up the tank, empty out the family and get right back to the trip. MacKremmon shrank, constricted and saw its luster fade. Over a period of years, young people moved away and businesses began to close; jobs dried up. By the time it was 125 years old, the town was returning to its own roots as a rustic, charming, dilapidated spot.

By the early 1990's, artists, poets, potters, furniture makers and writers from Boulder, Idaho Springs, Marble and Evergreen eventually heard about worn apartments and cheap rents. They moved their easels, chisels and wood lathes into run-down spacious studios and rented large, airy rooms. They painted the walls with the same attention they gave their canvases or their handmade jewelry. A hardware store opened to meet the needs for tools, lumber and hinges. A cooperative was formed and the old saloon was rehabbed, the original bar remained and shelves of hand painted ceramics lined the room; deep colored acrylics and pale watercolors hung on the rough, unsanded walls. A rich artist colony was shaping itself in MacKremmon.

Chapter Eight

In the following years, Reggie and I ate chili and lots of it as Daddy did his best to keep our little family together. Daddy was the only parent now and teacher conferences, field trips and holidays from school were important to him. He regularly lost a day's pay to spend time with us, take us to see Doc Hedstrum when we were sick, fly kites on a windy May afternoon. Daddy's love and caring had been an unremarked upon gift of comfort and I missed it when a sudden heart attack took him one Monday morning. I was 19.

Easily half of MacKremmon turned out for the memorial service after the cremation. Ladies of the Methodist Church put out platters of sandwiches and cookies. I must have eaten something but I don't remember tasting anything. All the men shook our hands and clapped us on the shoulder. The ladies hugged us and said things like, "You poor, sweet boys. Let me know if you need anything." As folks left, I found old Doc Hedstrum sitting on a folding chair.

"You doing ok, Ken?" he asked me.

"I guess. He loved us and he took good care of us. I guess it probably just wore him out," I replied.

"Your dad loved you and Reggie, Ken. But all those years of smoking probably caught up with him. His lungs just gave out. And he probably didn't do his heart any favors either. Cigarettes are hard on your health. And your dad went through a lot of stress, what with your mother leaving and him raising you two boys alone."

"Yeah," I said, "she just disappeared. We never knew what happened to her."

Doc Hedstrum's eyebrows were bushy as Johnson grass and they arched over his glasses like arthritic fingers. "Your dad was a quiet, private man, Ken. But he told me that he'd tried. He wrote letters to people in Georgia – any name he could remember that your mother may have mentioned - they were all sent back marked 'return to sender.' He even tried to get the Georgia State law enforcement to look for his car thinking he'd find her that way. But nothing worked. He loved her and he wanted you and Reggie to have a mother. He wanted to locate her, it just didn't turn out." The old doctor sighed and the lines in his face congregated into sagged pouches.

"Your dad always said Edie loved you boys as much as she could. He loved being your dad but having the sole responsibility of your care probably affected his health slowly, over the years. There was nothing to do for it. You and Reggie should be careful. You both need to quit smoking and learn how to handle stress."

"Yeah, well, I'm ok." I told him with more than a little teenage arrogance, "but I'm pretty sure Reggie doesn't think she loved him as much as she could."

Doc Hedstrum's head lifted and his crepey neck became straight in the starched white shirt collar; suddenly, it looked too big for him, cavernous around his thin neck. His chin lifted and he looked unusually stern.

"He will, Ken. He's angry now but give him time. He will."

By the time Mama left, the population of MacKremmon had grown to nearly 1,000 and every adult and most of the older children knew what had happened to us, "the Evans boys." Mama had always said that half the population knew the news, any news, by breakfast and the other half heard it by lunchtime. I expect the news of her leaving traveled at that speed, too. Neighbors expressed not exactly pity but a sense of appropriate soft attention. Probably the men felt pity at Chet's loss of the wife who cooked meals and took care of the house. And maybe the women wondered how one of their own sex had the courage, the blatant smarminess to just pick up and leave.

As news of Mama's departure spread through town faster than word of the circus coming, what Daddy called "the casserole brigade" of local ladies fed us for weeks. Most of the helpful ladies were married women expressing compassion and being neighborly. But a few were widows or single women and when they came by the house, they wore their prettiest dresses and bent down toward us, tilted their heads and spoke sweetly, almost musically.

For several weeks, Elise Langford made it a point to always chat casually with Daddy at church. Lollipops or bubble gum came out of her purse for us. Reggie and I always thanked her shyly.

"Miz Langford came all the way over here from Hygiene, Dad. She seems real nice," I said one night as we spooned up the last of the sauce in her homemade chicken potpie.

"Yeah, I'm sure she's a fine woman, Ken. I think I lack interest and energy in equal parts. She'll meet a nice man – but it won't be me."

Daddy sidestepped an in-person conversation by leaving the clean casserole dish on her front porch with a 'thank-you' note inside. After that, we noticed that Ms. Langford waved and smiled as she walked to her car after church.

As spring warmth bored into the ground and freed the

solid cold there, the three of us males gradually cooked and ate the remaining chickens, took down the wobbly chicken-wire fence and used the space for our work. Daddy had always repaired cars for friends, and now we had a space to work. We propped cars on cast-off crumbling cinder blocks there in the side yard and drained and replaced oil, changed timing belts, repaired radiators, recharged batteries. When dark came, we ran a long black cable from the kitchen window out to the car where it was hooked to the hood of the ailing vehicle. A light in a wire cage dangled under the hood, so we could work late into the dark.

After Daddy died, Reggie and I accepted fewer and fewer cars to work on and while we never really talked about it, we just continued to live in the house; it was our home. With or without our parents, it was all we knew.

For about five years after Daddy's death, the two of us, me lanky and serious and Reggie rounded and carefree, turned into young men with a common goal of maintaining ourselves as a family. Mama had taught us both how to make a bed, clean the house, shovel snow and fix a meal. In the summer, we mowed the yard and planted a few tomato plants. In the winter, we played cards and cribbage. When teenage Reggie went out with friends, I stayed at home focused on a car part that needed intense attention.

Reggie would tease me, "C'mon, go out with us. Live a little. No cute girl is going to come ring our doorbell. I'm going out lookin' for one to get up close with and you should, too."

"Naw, I think I'll stay here tonight. I can't leave Tooley – she might get lonely." I'd spread newspaper on the kitchen table where I could clean spark plugs with an old toothbrush or wind black electrical tape around a worn hose.

I knew that the county's social services were thinly stretched and I hoped we could stay just at the periphery of the wide examining eye of the agency. On the required visit of a

Grand County social worker, I coached Reggie and we radiated warm smiles and clean shirts for her. Our charm worked and kept the do-gooders from snagging Reggie, separating us, wiping out our little family. When Reggie reached 18 and finished high school, I felt pride, and a certain exhaling relief, as I watched the diploma flop with finality into my brother's hand.

I had gotten through high school with decent grades in math, English, American history and science. But the satisfaction I found in fixing cars, helping my buddies patch up their old jalopies after school and on weekends, was what kept me going. My reputation as a mechanic spread and guys would come from McCoy, Big Thompson Canyon and Pinewood Springs just to have me take a look at their cars.

Over the years, I had earned pocket money by sweeping the floor, emptying the trash and being the boy-janitor at Mac's, where Daddy had worked. I had spent after-school hours listening to the men talk about sickly vehicles and how to heal them; I absorbed it all. The guys at the garage may have looked rough and dark but they all knew me and kept a friendly eye on me. Del was the long-time manager and he always had a grin and a joke. Two weeks before my high school graduation, I asked for a full-time job.

"Come back the Monday after you move that tassel and we'll talk," Del told me. And he was good to his word. I put on navy blue twill pants and matching shirt – my new uniform - and went to work the week after graduation.

Years of hanging around with my dad and his friends had taught me how a car's engine works, what to look for when it doesn't. When I started working on a car, it was like everything else disappeared; my hands took over - knew what to do and just did it. I often found my mind following my hands, thinking through the problem not in cadence with the movement of those hands, but later, as if thinking was a step or two behind the manual dexterity of those two sensitive and articulated instruments at the end of my arms.

"It's like you have intelligent hands," Del said to me.

"I guess," I shrugged. "I like working on cars, it's what I know. My dad taught me."

"Yeah, he was the best. Toward the end, arthritis had started to slow him down," Del shook his head. "He was real proud of you, though."

I had worked at Mac's for nearly three years when Quik Lube, a national chain, showed an interest in the station. Auditors were sent out and for six weeks, they delved into each aspect of the garage, asked questions of the employees, measured the parking lot, chatted with the other merchants in town and scrutinized the books. Then Quik Lube made an offer.

Ed McNinch had owned the station for 32 years and now at age 67, he was ready to retire. His only son had come home from Korea with injuries that showed and some that didn't and he lived in a group home in Denver. Ed and his wife Frances wanted to give up home maintenance and be close to their son. A move to one of the patio homes being built in Denver's Aurora neighborhood made sense. Mac's Garage was sold and became a member of the Quik Lube chain. A bright red, white and green sign atop a pole went up in front of the garage.

Del agreed to stay on for two years, to help with the transition. After that, he'd take the buy-out package and retire.

"I've already got it planned. I'm gonna buy me a riding mower and a snowplow. Then I can stay outside all day, every day," he told me. "You come by anytime."

The nationwide parent company let a couple of the mechanics go but made a point of signing me on, even giving me a hiring bonus.

I like to think that Quick Lube recognized my ability to tinker with an engine and get it going; I was an asset. The company sent me to corporate headquarters in Minneapolis for orientation and training. The outline for the week of study included classes where I would hone my skills and get certified in oil change and transmission care.

I can't count how many times I'd said my closet could be an echo chamber, I had so few clothes. Before the trip to Minneapolis, Reggie and I drove to Sears in Winter Park where I bought a pair of dress pants and a couple of shirts. Two days later, Reggie drove me to the small airstrip outside Winter Park where the corporate plane would pick me up. As I got out of the car, Reggie reached over to the waistline of the new khaki slacks.

"Hey, bro, might want to take the tag off those pants."

I looked down and yanked off the white paper rectangle. I held it up to Reggie and said, "Here it is, the symbol of a new beginning."

I had no problem with the training, and actually enjoyed the eight hours a day of instruction in a classroom with nine other new Quik Lube employees. At night, all of us guys ate dinner together, saw some of Minneapolis and hunched over the notebooks to do our homework. We ended the week by agreeing to keep in touch.

"So how was the big city, bro?" Reggie asked when I returned to MacKremmon.

"It's cold and grey in Minneapolis – and the traffic is crazy. There are lots of buildings, some of'em at Riverside Plaza are so tall they start to look tilted at the top. I felt like a real hick from the sticks but I just stared and stared. They're talking about building a mall with a roller coaster and a hotel inside the mall." I looked at Reggie whose eyebrows rose like warm bread.

"I know. How would you ever feel like you belonged, had a special place in life in a city that big? Sometimes I wonder what it would be like to live in a big city. You ever think about living somewhere else?" I smoothed out the white paper napkin and lifted the fork and knife.

"Naw, not really. Sometimes I think about it but I'm happy." Reggie slid the white paper scabbard off the straw which went into his glass of water.

"I'd miss all this. I love the peacefulness of the woods and the mountains," I said.

"You must, you spend enough time hiking and camping." Reggie winked at the dark-haired waitress as she set our plates down in front of us. "Mama always said you had the scent of the wild on you from all the time you spent outdoors."

"Sometimes I think about what it would be like to leave MacKremmon. Remember Little Dickie Wilkerson? He's gone to Hollywood and changed his name to Rick Wilkes." I smiled at our waitress, and stuck a fork into green beans on my plate. "What do you think our lives would be like if we left here?"

"I don't know," Reggie mused. "And I wonder if I'll ever find out. I like living in our house and knowin' everybody in town. I like having Tooley around. I understand why Dickie – eh, I mean Rick – moved away. Remember when you two were in ninth grade and Greg Barstow and his big-muscled friends painted his locker pink? That wasn't the worse thing they did to him." Reggie looked down at the mashed potatoes on his plate. He raised an eyebrow and I nodded a tight-lipped frown. "Anyway, except for Rick who wanted another life, I'm not sure why people leave."

Celebrating with dinner at Deno's in Winter Park was a splurge. We both had steak, a rare treat, and choke cherry pie for dessert. Reggie was underage but he slurped down more than half of my three beers. Maybe I shouldn't have let him but we left satisfied and happy.

By the time I had worked in the MacKremmon Quik Lube for six months, the company discovered that I could do more than change filters and top up engine fluids – I could have told them that but it's probably better they found it out on their own. They said I had "a warm smile, polite manners" and while I thought I had an intense stare, my boss called it "clear-eyed charm." Since I'd grown up in the town, I knew everyone by name and I had no trouble talking to people. And when it came to cars, I knew what I was talking about.

"Hey, Mrs. Greeson, I made sure we replaced the gasket on the oil pan in your Buick. The threads on the old one had worn away. A new gasket keeps the drain plug on the pan secure." Mrs. Greeson might not know what the gasket was but she seemed to feel safe that I did and was watching out for her.

I remember saying, "When's that baby due, Lona Raye? I know you and Ed will make wonderful parents. You might want to get the shocks replaced because that's what helps you stop sooner. We gotta keep your Dodge in tip-top shape now that you're going to have a family riding in it." I loved cars and never forgot a detail and women customers especially seemed grateful, warmed to me. I needed that sense of being involved and valued.

The company enrolled me in correspondence marketing classes and promoted me to the front office. I had a new grey uniform shirt with my name stitched in red thread over the left pocket and I greeted each person who came through the door. In six months, business increased by twenty percent, a fact not lost on the Quik Lube bean counters.

Tooley had died in her sleep six weeks before Reggie graduated from Grand County High School. She was nearly sixteen years old and was so thin her whiskers were the widest part of her. Her meow came out "aakko" and her left ear was notched, evidence that at some point, she had barely escaped a fox.

Reggie was mechanically minded and after graduation, he got a job in maintenance, keeping two Winter Park ski lifts in perfect operating condition. Ski resorts had to be certified safe and mandatory inspections by a team from the State of Colorado were unannounced. Reggie's skill kept the equipment ready to meet rigorous requirements of the surprise visits. He liked the work and was well paid. He often said that skiing for free was "gravy on the biscuit." In addition to his salary, he had a rent-free one-bedroom apartment in back of Devil's Thumb Resort, near the ski supply shed.

Before Reggie moved out of the house, he pushed a large quartz stone out of the back of the pick-up and onto the spot under the cottonwood tree where Tooley was buried. He wiped his shirtsleeve across his eyes.

"Allergies."

"Yeah," I nodded, "me, too."

He tossed two cardboard boxes full of his clothes into the back of the truck. Then he walked back to the big rock. He squatted next to it, rested on hand on it and bowed his head for just a moment.

"You were a good cat, Tooley.

Then he got in the truck and drove off. I waved but he didn't look back.

While the slopes and lifts were idle in the summertime, Reggie was the general handyman at Devil's Thumb and Beaver Creek Condos which hosted up to 125 families during ski season and groups of hikers and bird watchers in snow-less weather. It sometimes meant a middle-of-the-night call to unclog a toilet or provide a lost key, but Reggie didn't mind.

Reggie was easy about life and he loved being around people. He spent hours, both elbows leaning on the bar, laughing and chatting with visitors and locals alike. Winter or not, there were plenty of skiers and tourists who laughed at his stories and bought rounds. He often joked that if he could keep his clean clothes behind the bar, he'd never need to go home. The whole arrangement suited him just fine.

Chapter Nine

I OFTEN THOUGHT ABOUT WOMEN but in a dream-like way, as if they were in some distant hazy location, under a sign saying "Not Available – For You!" or some other discouraging banner. I knew I was in the real world and my arms were not long enough to reach into the gauzy, mysterious imaginary haze. I felt like I couldn't get up close to a woman – until Noreen.

Noreen Horn was tall, about five feet eight, just right for my six-foot-one-inch height. She was slim and poised, perfectly comfortable in her own skin. Her shoulders rounded over just a little and her backbone bumped out like a vertical column of interspersed knuckles denting the zipped-up back of the pale yellow cotton dress she wore almost every day. I can't remember exactly when we met, I just know she was there, hanging around Quik Lube where I was now the manager.

Noreen's skin was clear and fair and healthy looking, not chalky and pale like some of the local girls. She had a medium forehead on her heart-shaped face, and bones that lifted warm, rosy-toned cheeks up and out, as if they were three-dimensional rounds. I was fascinated by watching the smooth, even-toned skin on her hands. There were no blemishes; no dark nicotine stains like I remember on Mama's hands. Her eyes were as brown as piled late-autumn leaves.

On Monday, Wednesday and Friday she left her desk as dispatcher for the Grand County Sheriff's office and brought lunch to her brother Ray who worked Bay #2, alignment and transmissions. Noreen would tell Ray the chicken sandwich with cheese was "*cordon bleu*" or she would call the lettuce "*on-deev*" instead of *endive*. If she and Ray disagreed on any random topic, she'd say, "Let's don't air our *contretemps* here."

I used to tease her that the only French words I knew were "French fry" and "Chevrolet Coupe" and I pronounced it "cou-pay." She always gave me a frosting-fluffy little laugh and the way she flashed me a glance made her seem a little shy, a little removed, a little apart. Each look seemed to carry a hint of intimacy that made me swallow silently, a little embarrassed that I'd noticed.

Abner, Ray, Noreen and me - we all sat together at the splintery picnic table out back. The benches were attached to the wooden table at the base and Noreen had to swing her legs over, one at a time, to sit down. Her legs were shapely, smooth looking and seemed to dangle from the hem of her dress. I had to remind myself it was rude to stare at those gorgeous limbs. I had to make myself look away.

It got to where noontime, lunchtime, was my favorite time of day. Noreen would lift her perfectly cut sandwich from neatly creased waxed paper, gaze right into my eyes, answer my sometimes stammered questions and ask me some in return. She almost always brought potato salad or brownies or homemade bread-and-butter pickles to share.

She had a long, graceful neck and I loved the way her straight, chin-length hair seemed anchored in the crown of her perfectly shaped head. Strands of gold like sunlight glinting on the creek interspersed the brown ones. Her hair swung forward when she lowered her head and nodded toward me. It looked like a thick, heavy curtain, one that I wanted to enclose just the two of us, and keep the rest of the world out. Her hair was what I thought of a million times a day; *her hair, oh, her hair.*

The summer ended like wind whooshing past the windows of a speeding car. One October Thursday, Ray and I found ourselves alone at the outdoor picnic table.

"Want some?" I was suddenly nervous and pushed a single-serving bag of potato chips toward Ray.

"Naw, thanks," Ray replied. He looked down at chinks in the rough wooden table and smoothed out the wrinkles in a small brown paper bag. The fall weather was sunny but chilly and he pulled his lightweight jacket closer at the neck. "So you and Reggie doin' ok?"

"Yeah, we're great. Not much bothers Reggie." I paused and inhaled. "You and your sister share an apartment, right?" I watched Ray nod. "Are your parents still living? You two the only kids?" I had both elbows on the table and I tried to sound casual. I picked a salted yellow chip out of the packet. I held it up, looked at it and put it on the rough table.

"Yeah. Our dad died some years ago. I was thirteen but Noreen was only nine. I did okay, sort of knew I was the man of the house and I helped my mom a lot. Mom had never worked, she'd always taken care of us, and with Dad gone, there was no money coming in. I was old enough to mow lawns and shovel snow but Noreen took it really hard. She didn't like not having things." Ray took a bite of banana and chewed.

"I'm not gonna lie to you, it was a rough time. Meeker is a small town and once the little bit of insurance money gave out, we had to go on food stamps and everyone knew it. It was temporary but boy, it was tough on Noreen. By the time she was a junior, she was dating Alex Huntley. His dad owns the Oldsmobile dealership in Winter Park. I don't know if she ever really cared for him but he bought her nice things and took her places. Before Noreen graduated, Mom was working at

Rocky Mountain Quilts, that trendy little shop that moved to downtown Grand Lake last year, you know the one?"

I blinked and semi-nodded.

"But Noreen felt like Elaine O'Hotto and Janet McElroy and all the other girls had Gap clothes and Swatch watches and things she didn't. Hell, you know what girls are like."

"Not really," I shook my head. "It's just Reggie and me. Clothes are something we wear while we work on cars."

"Yeah, I hear you. But girls can be tough on each other. So Noreen, on purpose, didn't make a lot of close friends in high school. As soon as she graduated, she dropped Alex, left Meeker and moved here. We've got a two-bedroom apartment over on 4th Street and Mohawk and it works for us. She's got her job at the sheriff's office and I think she kind of likes being dispatcher. She feels like people can't see her, can't judge her by how she looks." Ray gathered the floppy yellow pieces of banana peel by the bottom and folded them together to form a hollow upside-down shell.

"Mom took it hard, felt like she had sort of failed Noreen. But Noreen's doing great now. I think she's starting to forgive Mom. And Mom's getting over some of the guilt." Ray exhaled and scratched his ear.

"Mmmm, I can understand all that." I crumpled the empty potato chip bag in my right hand and then pried it open with the fingers of my left hand. "Our mother left Reggie and me – it's no secret. I guess everybody in town knows the story of our lives. Whether your parent dies or just walks out, it's tough. It's like when a car throws a rod, even when it's fixed, it changes things." I got up to toss the mangled shiny bag into the oil barrel trash can.

I didn't want to look like I was nervous-shaking so I propped against the doorjamb. With my right hand, I pulled the six-point socket wrench out of my shirt pocket. Then nervously, pushed it back into the same space. My hands suddenly felt useless. They became fists and shoved their way into my pants pockets.

"Your sister is really good looking and well, she doesn't have a boyfriend, does she?" My shoulders rose involuntarily like I was defending myself against a negative answer.

Ray grinned and tilted his chair onto its two back legs.

"She says you're 'cute.' I think I'm supposed to pass that information along at just the right time." He put his interlaced fingers behind his head and grinned. I nodded and turned so Ray couldn't see my pleased look as I eased myself back to work.

The next couple of weeks passed in a blur of long workdays as the locals got their vehicles ready for winter. Lunches were the high-beam spots in the weeks for me.

It was a clear cold November Wednesday, two weeks before Thanksgiving. Snow was piled shivering on the wooden table outside so Ray, Noreen, Abner and I were sitting at the yellow 1950s chrome-edge Formica table. The garage's break room was windowless but chilly enough that Noreen had on a bulky navy blue ski sweater over her cotton dress. The talk turned to Hollywood's latest blockbuster, *Star Wars.*

"I hear Carrie Fisher does a great acting job in it," Ray said.

"Acting? Who cares if she can act – she's gorgeous," Abner said. He screwed the top back onto the thermos. Lunch had been his wife's homemade vegetable soup, his favorite, and it always left him in a good mood. He and Ray scraped their chairs back and stood up. Still laughing and discussing Princess Leia, they threw away closely bitten apple cores and aluminum foil, defenseless against the crumpling, as they went back to work.

"We should go see it," I said to Noreen once we were alone, "*Star Wars*, the movie. How 'bout Saturday night?" I looked down and slid the bread crusts, the remainder of my peanut butter and jelly sandwich, around with my index finger.

"Sure," Noreen said. "Just us or are Ray and Abner going,

too?"

I immediately cracked a smile and my eyes crinkled with it. My head perked up and I looked into Noreen's eyes; the sense of intimacy was strong as juice through jumper cables.

"Hey, I know it's taken me awhile to ask you out. You have to cut me a little slack here."

Noreen's smile relaxed its way across her face and I felt the muscles in my chest ease, felt my shoulders rise slightly as if hope buoyed them.

"Let's do the early show. I'll pick you up at six."

A light dusting of snow made the sidewalk sparkle and people huddle in their coats. But the appeal of *Star Wars* was strong and a line had formed at the Silver Screen Cinema in Winter Park. We had gotten there early, before every seat filled up, and Noreen directed us toward a seat half way down in the middle of the row.

"The perfect spot," she said, "I like to be right in the middle of things."

As Luke Skywalker was piloting the spaceship and dodging the Death Star's laser beams, she squealed, "Ohhh, Kenny!" and gripped my arm. For a split second, I thought she might end up in my lap. It made me feel larger, broader, needed. I put my arm around Noreen and pulled her closer.

Afterwards, we drove east to Grand Lake and ate at Dougal's Mountain Inn. There, in the gift shop, we found a plaque that read "*Laissex les bons temps rouler*." I bought it for Noreen.

"Maybe that'll be our motto. 'Let the good times roll.'" I tried to sound casual.

Just a week later, on our second date, we drove to Steamboat Springs where we ate in the new Italian restaurant. Elsie and Chuck Taylor, the new owners, had named it Taylor Made Pizza. Each table sported a red and white checked tablecloth and a candle in a wine bottle heavy with dripped wax.

"Creates a warm, romantic ambiance in this chilly weather, don't you think?" the hostess asked. The place was small and unpretentious for a Steamboat restaurant but it radiated charm. Piped-in Motown music and a noise-bubbling crowd added to the comfort. When the Taylors found out it was our second date, they insisted that we have a bottle of Chianti on the house.

"You're a cute couple," Elsie said to us. "I bet you'll be happy together."

I grinned and nodded and watched her pour wine into each of our glasses.

"Thanks," I meant it, "that's really nice." I couldn't help notice that Noreen showed a tight-lipped smile and her eyelashes fluttered but she didn't blush. She took just a sip of wine.

We talked about the movie as I drove her home.

"Come on in. I'll make some tea," Noreen said. "Ray had to go change the light bulb on Mother's front porch and he's spending the night there."

We were barely inside the small apartment when Noreen kissed me. It took only seconds for surprise to turn to released longing. My fingers spread out and both hands slipped themselves, like an explorer in a strange country that he knows well, into Noreen's hair. It was thick and my hands felt the weight of it, the pressure yet lightness of it all – *like heavy marshmallows*, I thought. The stupidness of it all made me pull my face away, look at her and smile and immediately kiss her again, my hands never freeing themselves, never wanting to free themselves from the snowbroth, the cotton fleece, the Christmas angelhair, the soft heaviness that was her hair.

When I realized I'd need my hands to unzip the yellow cotton dress, I took them out of her hair, lowered the zipper and the lightweight dress fell to the floor. Noreen unbuttoned the first two buttons on my best plaid shirt.

"Too slow," I told her. My arm went up, bent at the

elbow and I reached my hand to the back of the collar. I yanked the still mostly buttoned shirt up and over my head and tossed it onto the floor.

"I've never seen anyone take off a shirt that way!" Noreen laughed.

Our clothes lay in a comfortable jumble on the floor beside Noreen's bed. I wanted to explore every square inch of her body – the soft, unblemished skin that fit all the round parts so snugly that my hands glided over each one – her breasts, her shoulders, her belly, her thighs. But her hair, I kept returning to her hair. It was where I buried my face, my hands, the male sounds I made in the process. I was surprised at how natural and unhurried the lovemaking was, how gently but intensely I peaked and how easy the inevitable sighing afterglow was.

Afterwards, lying close together on the double bed, I was propped up on two pillows and Noreen lay on her left side, facing away from me. She rolled over to her back and I looked down onto her clear skin.

My left index finger traced a line from the center of her lower lip, fuller than her upper lip, down her chin, down the glowing skin on her neck and ended at the hollow at the base of her throat. I had looked at that spot a thousand times and the concave look, the shape of it always reminded me of a handleless spoon bowl. The skin dipped inward, not sinking but relaxing, lolling confidently and gently toward Noreen's interior. Now my fingertip gently eased its way around the scoop, gently brushing that slight basin, the dip, the bottomless hollow. I fell into it.

I lifted a strand of Noreen's glorious weighty hair out of her eyes and twirled it between index finger and thumb. I watched the lock as it fell onto the pillow. I kissed her forehead. I drew back and stared at her. I felt my breath catch in my throat and I had to swallow. I felt like the air had gone out of me, not in a *whoosh* like it exits a balloon but gently loosed from my body and elongated softly into the atmosphere. I lay back, empty of breath, not sagging but almost weightlessly swaying as if I were in a hammock eased by a light-touch breeze. I felt the sweet spot of divine emptiness that comes just at the split second before the next breath must be drawn. I was suspended, gliding without movement, without weight, without form.

My mind went back to when I was eight and a half and Reggie was a toddler. The whole family was headed to Denver to see Daddy's cousin Cal in a car show. Reggie and I were in the backseat of the Chevy, slipping around on the seat like link sausages on a greasy plate. As the car turned from State Road 40 and banked left onto Highway 34, it slowed in its climb. At that spot, the top of the incline cut off our view of the downhill side of the road, like a picture folded shows a flat, even line and nothing beyond. Above the sharp black horizon line was sky – no road ahead was in sight. It looked like the car would pull up to the sharp line and stop, teetering there, before the wheels met the clouds.

Daddy and Mama were in the front seat. The car coughed and Daddy glanced at Mama, "She's having trouble with this hill."

"She'll make it," Mama told him. "She knows we're off on a family adventure and she'll make it." She grinned easily, casually as if she didn't care whether they made it or not and ran her fingers through hair just behind her ear.

In the back seat, our little-boy commotion stopped. We slumped back against the seat, elbows tucked and arms at our sides, silent. Each of us seemed to inhale and then freeze. There was that vaporous moment, that sweet hollowness, that dazzling second of light when no one moved. Listening to the car motor work at the climb was the only sound. The air was still.

The car did indeed get to the top of the hill and at that sudden instant, we all talked and laughed and breathed out. Our shrill giggles and lightweight words filled the back seat. Daddy looked at Mama, "You were right. She made it."

The chaotic chatter lasted only a few seconds until the descent snapped the pace. As young as we were, we felt it, too. The car seemed suspended, hammock-swaying in space as it began the downhill glide. The engine seemed to quiet itself and the vehicle eased down as slowly as if it had not meet the asphalt under it. Daddy had taken his foot off the gas pedal and the car was under its own power. We were suspended, winging on a frequency so high it was without vibration, mute. As it rushed in the wind, mottled green flashes went by the windows. With a feeling of slow motion, the car seemed to float. When the Chevy reached the flat part of the road with a soft *thunp*, Reggie and I looked at each other. Our widened eyes began to relax and ease; our chests collapsed with a sigh. In my memory, the sense of awe had been stretched out, elongated. No one had spoken for a long second.

I felt that sense of suspended wonder now as I blinked and looked at Noreen. I wanted to be a superhero who could freeze the moment, wanted to wrap my invisible cape around us and have that exquisite suspended teetering never end. My mind wanted to close itself around the moment, the perfect satisfied mystery moment.

Noreen got up, pulled on a red and black silk robe and stepped to the stove to make hot tea. As water heated in the kettle, she opened the drawer for spoons. Suddenly, she leaned over the sink and threw up.

"Was the veal scaloppini bad?" I jumped up out of bed and grabbed up my boxer shorts, putting a leg in with each step as I stretched to the sink. I held Noreen's thick hair away from her face and reached for a wet dishcloth. Noreen shook her head and held her hand out for the cool fabric comfort. I guided her elbow as she sat down in one of the wooden ladder-back chairs.

"No, the food was all right." She paused. I inhaled and this breath felt real to me again. I blinked a couple of times.

"Ken, I'm pregnant."

I felt my head jerk upright on my neck and for a few seconds, my serious gaze must have bored into her. She looked directly at me and then her eyelashes fluttered down like a delicate innocent branch, laden with snow, snaps soundlessly and falls forever from the tree. She tucked a thick, weighty lock of hair behind her left ear and moved her eyes to the kitchen table. Even her eyelashes looked suddenly pale.

"What? Huh?" I needed something to do with my hands. I stared at the spigot. I turned on the faucet and watched the water rush around the sink.

"I am. I'm about two and a half months along."

"But we've only … I mean …" I took the dishcloth from her, ran it under the flowing faucet and turned the water off again. I used both hands to give the cloth a strong twist and handed it to her without thinking.

"I know." She patted the wet cloth onto her now colorless forehead and then brushed the coolness up her hairline. "I know."

"What? Ohmigod, Noreen. Are you ok? A baby … what do you … uh, how will you … I mean, what are your plans?"

"I ... I don't know right now. Most of the time, I'm feeling too queasy to think much about it. Some days, I have morning sickness *and* night-time sickness." She tried for a straight-line little smile. Her cheekbones had lost their dimension, and looked flat in her now colorless face.

I was frozen in place and hadn't sat down. She glanced up at me.

"Ray thinks I should do something about it. He knows a doctor in Gunnison."

She blotted her forehead three times with the cool cloth. "But Mother wants me to go on and have the baby. I just don't think I could do it alone. I don't know." She folded her arms on the tabletop and leaned over to rest her forehead on them. Layers of her thick hair fell forward and hid her face. "I just don't know."

" I uh, I've got to have a cigarette. I'll call you," I mumbled. I patted her back in an awkward, step-back gesture of comfort. My arms and legs seemed loose, disjointed like they were stammering as I struggled into my clothes.

The road was straight outside the windshield but my thoughts swirled and twisted. They battled to break free and arrange themselves in sensible order. I drove awhile and then went off the main road and onto a bumpy dirt path. When I got to the wide spot near the Springs, I pulled off. As I turned off the ignition, I could hear laughter and shrieking coming from Hot Strawberry Springs.

It was the local hangout, the spot where older teens and twenty-somethings enjoyed the natural hot water spa for free after the attraction closed on Labor Day. In daylight hours, everyone wore a swimsuit or cut-offs. But in the dark, clothing was optional and most swimmers were nude. Flickers of bodies shone in the moonlight as it moved on the small sight. The crowd and noise would both have been bigger in the summertime but for the little group who braved convention and the autumn cold, it was a risqué Saturday night adventure. For some, almost a rite of passage.

I lit a cigarette and thought about the first time I went skinny dipping at the Springs. I was with Little Dickie who immediately disappeared with a group of guys. I was nearly sixteen and my chest and bicep muscles were developing. Christy Newman was seventeen and she glanced at me several times. After splashing awhile with a crowd, Christy walked up to me, took my hand and led the way to a dark spot between two tall rocks. She lay down on our towels and pulled me to her. It was my first time and it didn't last long but when we got up, I remember I was shaking all over. I wasn't sure what to do next but Christy kissed me hard on the mouth. "Ahhh," she said and walked back to join her friends. I rubbed my arms to stop shaking but I couldn't stop grinning.

On Monday at school, I knew I'd see Christy. I had wrung my hands, felt my eyebrows sweating with trying to think what to say. When she appeared, I managed, "Uhh …" But Christy barely batted her eyes in my direction, gave a shake of her head as a weak as a leaf in the early spring. She kept her focus and her pace as she passed me and joined her friends. She did not look at me or speak to me the rest of the school year and when she graduated, she moved to Wyoming where her older sister lived.

Until this moment, the thought of that first sexual experience had always come to my mind when I visited – or even thought of – the Springs. I'd always felt a firming, an arousing physical reaction to the memory. But not tonight.

Tonight, the chilly aloneness suited me; I didn't want to talk to anyone. The woods were too dark and cold to walk in. But being surrounded by them, snuggled into their brittleness, seemed to take the pressure off my rapid heartbeat. I sat there in the car parked lopsided on the edge of the road, a part of the dark, for a long time. Voices from the Springs began to fade, grow quiet and muted and far away.

My neck relaxed and my head lolled back. Behind my eyelids, I saw Mama. She'd been gone for nearly fifteen years but she looked like the young woman of my childhood. Without warning, Noreen appeared and I was standing next to her. Children surrounded us – tall boys with dark hair and serious eyes, girls with high, rosy cheekbones, dressed in yellow cotton dresses. I realized I was watching my mother's face and the muscles in her temples relaxed as her eyes widened and her mouth formed and "Oh." Her head turned slowly from side to side to see Noreen and the children. Maybe it was a reflection of the yellow dresses but I saw a circlet of pale gold, a frail, fluffy crowning around her head. As her head turned toward me, her lips smoothed themselves into a sweet, even line. Her eyes found me and her look said, "You did it. That's my boy." Then the features of her face – eyebrows, eyes, nose, lips – and the weightless pale cloud vanished. Choppy grey smoke came from the side and engulfed her head, her lamb's wool hair – and then her entire figure.

Sharp shrieks came from the Springs. My eyes opened. I sat up straight in the driver's seat, blinked several times. Then I re-started the car's engine and drove home.

I couldn't sleep and as the stars rolled up into the sky and horizontal striations of salmon-colored dawn showed at the mountaintops, I called in for the first time ever.

"You ok? Are you sick or something?" I could hear Del take a big gulp of coffee.

"Naw, I just got a lot on my mind. I need some time to think. And I know you get up early."

"Yeah, working in a garage will do that for ya. What can I do for you, Ken? Is there anything wrong? Is Reggie ok? Is it girl trouble?"

I knew the men at the garage had watched the awkward courtship and I figured that's why Del had asked the question.

"Well, yeah, I guess you could say that. She's really beautiful." I couldn't speak for just a few seconds. "But I just don't know what I want, what I ought to do, what I *want* to do."

"It's none of my business, 'a course, but I've known you and Reggie your whole lives. Hell, I helped you loosen your first lugnut, didn't I?"

"Hmm …" My sigh verbalized itself.

"I'm here to tell you that falling in love is not for the lily-livered. You can grind down those gears worrying about it. Look, Ken, there are folks who spend years on a psychiatrist's couch or thousands of dollars on drugs, tryin' to get over their childhoods – their daddy hit them or their mama called them names. The truth is, you can't change anything that's happened to you, ever, no matter how hard you try, how bad you want to.

What happened to you or me or any of us is finished. Worrying over it's about as useless as a man standing in the female hygiene aisle of the drugstore." I heard Del take another sip of coffee.

"The choice is to go on, straight ahead down that new road. If you have a chance to be happy, you forget everything that's happened to you, wipe the past off your windshield so you can see the road clear ahead, open up the engine and go for it."

"Yeah, you make a lot of sense. I know a whole lot more about cars than I know about life and women. It's a lot to think about."

"No doubt about that," Del said. "You take the day off and figure it out. You come from strong stock, Ken."

"I'll see you tomorrow. Thanks, Del." I hung up and thought about nothing except Noreen and the words she had said.

I paced back and forth on the worn braided rug in the house where I'd grown up, ran my fingers through my hair, sat down, put my hands on my knees, got up again, asked questions and heard myself answer them. Jumbles of words rattled around in my head, echoed like tourists yelling down the walls of Deer Creek Canyon.

I called Reggie, woke him up, so I could hear myself say the words out loud, organize the sounds into logical, sequential word patterns that made some kind of sense.

"Whaa … whosit?" I knew Reggie had probably dropped into bed only a couple of hours before the phone woke him. "Kenny, everything ok? Talk to me, bro."

Reggie's personality was always upbeat and even the way he asked the question now sounded relaxed and easy-going, like he was. It took me three full minutes and four cigarettes to tell Reggie the story.

"You'd be giving up your bachelorhood."

"Yeah, right. I was always such a big partyer."

"I dunno, man," Reggie said. "Hang on a minute, would

you? I gotta go release some processed beer." I heard the toilet flush and then Reggie came back to the conversation. "You know I'm gonna be there with you in anything you want to do." He paused and I thought I could hear Reggie scratching his head as he tried to find a response.

"But good god, Kenny, are you sure? Mama was pregnant when she and Daddy got married and you saw how that turned out. I mean, think about it, bro. Noreen's gonna have a baby - someone else's baby. Trying to build a family out of that is like trying to rebuild an engine and putting in parts that you don't know where they came from."

I could hear the agitation in Reggie's voice. "Why doesn't she just marry the other guy? There's bound to be a guy in this story somewhere – why didn't she stay with him? Do you feel like she just run off and left him? Is that the kind of woman she is? Or did he leave Noreen and the baby? What about that? Does it make any difference to you?"

"I know what you're getting at, Reggie. We were left and you wonder how anyone could do that, if Noreen is the kind of person who would do that." For a second, there was dead silence on the line and I knew boyhood memories were expanding in the spotlight of each of our minds.

"I guess Mom had her reasons. She used to hug us close and say, 'I love you better'n snuff on a banana.' We didn't know what snuff was but it didn't matter," I told him.

"Do you remember the Seipp family who ran that big dude ranch in Muggins' Gulch when we were kids?" Reggie asked. "Wayne was in your class at school and Charlene was in mine."

"Yeah," I coughed. "Mama and Daddy sometimes played cards with their parents."

"Yeah," Reggie went on with his thought. "They were always like the perfect family. And they were taking the kids to Disneyland when the car crashed. All four of them were killed."

Reggie paused and swallowed hard. "There were times I almost wished that had happened to us – that we'd all died together - rather than us being left."

The sorrow seemed to stretch itself taunt on the line. My shoulder held the receiver to my ear. I lit a cigarette and clicked the lighter shut.

"I know," I said through pursed lips as I exhaled grey smoke, "but you and Daddy and me, we managed. Over the years, I've spent a lot of time in the woods, staring into campfires, sleeping next to streams and wondering about Mama. I finally got to the point of thinking that she really did love us, she just had her own demons to battle, like Dad said. We'll probably never know exactly what they were.

"But loving Mama doesn't mean I have to build my whole life around those feelings. I mean, look how Daddy handled it. Some mornings, he looked like he could barely drag himself around. Then he'd feed Tooley and start breakfast. It was like he gradually increased his speed and got going. And he did that every day." I felt purposeful as I ground out the Camel in the ashtray on the kitchen counter.

"I think I love Noreen. And it's almost like I need to trust Noreen to prove that I'm not going to let my life be decided by Mama's leaving us. I want to be in the driver's seat of my own life. I want a full life, a good life – and that includes a family." I lit another cigarette. I puffed a loud, smoke-filled exhale.

"I've thought a lot about this and I don't want to miss out on trusting someone, being close to someone, feeling secure in someone's soul because both of us, you and I, were abandoned and hurt. For years, I blamed myself for Mama's leaving, wondered what I could have done to make her stay.

"Then for several years after that, I felt like a car that had been in a bad accident, like I had a hardened dent in the fender that nothing could straighten out. I felt like it was my fault, at least partly, somehow – like, if I'd been somebody different, had done things different, maybe she wouldn't have left." I took another puff. Neither of us spoke.

"Well, that's just not so. Mama had to do what she had to do. It's almost like she left a family that we just happened to be in, you know? Like it happened that way because that's the way it was meant to be. Does that make any sense?" I could hear Reggie's regular breathing. "And for years, I felt like I wasn't worth much, like what I thought or who I was, didn't matter. If my own mother couldn't love me, I couldn't understand how anybody would be interested in me."

"What?" Surprise was in Reggie's voice. "Kenny, baby, you were the shit. Any guy who had a problem with his car would drive a hundred miles just to ask you to take a look at it. You know cars like nobody's business. Everybody wants to meet you. Man, you're still the best known mechanic in this part of Colorado." Reggie paused. "I've always been proud of you. You were always the 'do-right' guy. If a sign on the road said, 'Left lane closed in one mile,' you immediately got in the right lane. Me, I'd race up to the front of the line and wave and wink at the nearest woman driver. I'd charm her into letting me cut in and get ahead of everybody else.

"You remember the year we were the three wise men in the Christmas pageant? We had on bathrobes and Mom and Mrs. Fullenwider had made our cardboard crowns. You acted just like a wise man. Me, I hooked a candy cane through my crown and walked down the aisle of the church with the red and white stripes sticking straight up. That's just how I was.

"But you, Kenny, it seemed like you were always serious, you always took on the big jobs, like you were trying to prove your worth, and kind of earn attention. I was the goof off. I always felt like the oddball in our family. I never felt like I fit in. Daddy talked about taking us camping and I know he used to take you but did you notice he never took me? And it wasn't just that. I didn't look like you or Daddy. I always felt different.

I guess that's why I did so many stupid things. How many times did I hit you with that brass-knuckles red sock? You never squealed on me. I took more than my share of screwball chances. Do you remember that after the senior prom, I worried for nearly a month that Cassandra Scholl was knocked up? I chase women, drink too much and stay in trouble of one kind or another." Both of us were quiet for a moment.

"But, hey, this isn't about me. It's about you and your life and you deserve the best out of it. Having a family is great but c'mon, Kenny, is this really how you want to do it? I mean, it's not like fixing a flat tire, bro. You can't just put a patch on it and pump it full of air and get going. You're talkin' about a humdinger of a road trip here, a lifetime journey. You get that, right?"

"Reggie, you're the best brother I could have asked for. Daddy and Mama both loved you. I believe in my heart that they loved us both. We can't change a single thing about the past. I've always dreamed that I'd get married and have a family and that Mama would approve and somehow, I know she does. And our job now, as grown men is to have happy lives. That's what I want that, a good, solid life, a regular, everyday life."

We both knew the discussion was leading to a conclusion, one in which the strength of two wills, the views of both our psyches had to be acknowledged, honored, respected.

"Noreen needs me and I'm going do all I can for her – and the baby. Yeah, that's what I'm going do. I have to forget a lot of the past 'cause I can't change a single minute of it. I have to let go of a lot of old feelings. I don't want to spend my life in the past. I want to be with Noreen. I think we can be happy together. I think we can be a family, a real family, one for the long haul." I blew cigarette smoke out with a *whoosh* and a sigh.

There was quiet on the other end of the line.

"And I hope you'll be happy for me."

Reggie still didn't say anything.

"Right now, it's not important to me who the baby's

father is. Maybe some day she'll tell me. And maybe she won't. I've got a good job and I want a normal life. I think I'm ready to be a husband. And I'll figure out how to be a dad."

"Whew," Reggie gave a long exhale and it sounded like he'd been holding his breath, "a kid. It's a big responsibility. I hear what you're saying, Kenny, and I hope you're not trying to talk yourself into it." There was more silence and then Reggie said, "I can't really say I'm in favor of it, bro, I know I wouldn't do it. I mean, do you really know Noreen? And I know you want to be a husband and a dad – what does Noreen want? And you don't have to prove that you can hold a family together – what if you can't? Then what? Mama's not here to see you and there are no trophies for this." The silence fairly buzzed in my ear this time. I could almost hear the smoke from my cigarette curling its way toward the ceiling and beyond into the black.

"But we're brothers, we're all we've got. And if stepping up to this is what you want, I'm gonna be there for you."

Chapter Ten

I FELT LIKE MY EMOTIONAL GEARS had willingly been shoved into 'drive.' I think my feelings registered the commitment, even before the brain-generated certainty took hold of the thought process. The image in my mind of me standing behind the banner now saw my hand reach up, close around it and crush it. That barrier was gone. I had forged through the hazy unknown and here I was, in spite of Reggie's doubts, laying a claim to happiness. The one thing I wanted was in my grasp. The closeness, the solid unity of a family brushed the knuckles of the hand that gripped the banner. I thought of it as a way of standing up as a man, of passing along the love I'd learned from my father, sharing that same strong paternal connection and devotion.

I'm a grown man and I've got a good job. I've always wanted to feel like part of a family again and this seems like as good a time as any, I thought. I may not have planned it this way but I know it'll work. Noreen's a year older than I am and she'll be a good mom and we're both old enough to be responsible. I felt like I was fitting into the role, putting my arms in each sleeve and pulling it close, rather than having it thrown around me, weighted onto me. I took a deep breath and dialed Noreen's number.

"I want us to get married," I said when she answered.

"Are you sure?" Noreen asked. Her voice sounded wispy and ungrounded, like she hadn't been asleep.

"Yeah," I puffed on the cigarette in my hand. "Yeah, I'm sure."

"You're a great guy, Ken. You know you don't have to do this."

"Look, Noreen, I'm crazy about you, you know I am. I was a little scared of you at first because you're beautiful and you speak French. But we know each other now and we can make this work. After my mother left, I missed being part of a family. My dad was great and Reggie and I are close but it wasn't the same without a mother. I missed having a complete family. I've always known that I want to be in a family, a whole one. I know that nobody's family is perfect and that's ok with me. I want to be in a family whatever that brings with it. It's what I want, I'm sure it is." I took an inhale and exhaled thin smoke. "And if it's what you want, too, we can do this. We can make it work. It might be messy at times but it'll all be fine."

Colorado law says a marriage can be officiated by a court magistrate, a retired judge of a court, a public official whose powers include the solemnization of marriages or by the parties to the marriage themselves. I wanted it all to be official and Noreen said she did, too. I called the Grand County courthouse in Hot Sulfur Springs and that's where we were married.

The week before, Noreen and her mother Sheila had driven to Denver. Sheila told me later that they started at Foley's with Noreen trying on five dresses; none was just right. At Nordstrom's, Noreen picked out a stunning chemise-style dress.

"It's just a little snug," Sheila told me she had suggested it gently, "do you want to try the next size? You'll be a little bigger by the time the ceremony happens."

"No," Noreen had told her flatly, "I like this one and I'm

getting it. That's all there is to it, Mother."

The dress's heavy cream color made Noreen's brown eyes and blush-highlighted cheekbones stand out even more. I couldn't believe how beautiful she was.

"You look like a million dollars," I told my bride.

"Good," she replied with an amused smile and tiny wink, "that's just about what I spent on this dress."

As I handed her a bouquet of baby's breath and three pink roses from the florist in Winter Park, I thought I noticed a flash of disappointment crowding her eyebrows.

"I guess I was thinking of white cymbidium orchids," Noreen said as she looked down at the flowers. "They're more of a wedding flower."

"I figured that since your mom thinks it's a little girl, pink roses would have some, you know, meaning for us." I kind of stammered it out. My nervousness was seeping into my voice.

"It's a lovely bouquet," Noreen clamped her mouth in a closed-lip smile. One hand gripped the bouquet and the other found my calloused hand.

Herbert Cozens had been Grand County Justice of the Peace for over thirty years and he was dapper in a three-piece tweed suit, a pale blue shirt and a dark blue rep stripe necktie. He looked like he could have been a US Senator or judge, I thought. He told us he was planning to retire soon and our wedding was one of the last ceremonies he would perform.

"So this is a very special occasion," he told our little group, "for me as well as for Ken and Noreen." Noreen and I, the bride and groom, stood in front of a wooden podium, we held each other's hands and said, "I do," at the right moments. We exchanged rings Noreen had chosen, a plain gold band for me and a platinum band with four small diamonds for her.

"I now pronounce you man and wife," Mr. Cozens said. "You may kiss the bride." Noreen and I leaned toward each other and kissed gently. Then I looked at my wife and, in a moment of sheer joy, grinned and threw my arms around her. It caught Noreen off guard and she giggled.

"Don't see that every day in here," the Justice told us with a grin as he handed us each a pen. Signing the marriage certificate was proof of the marriage; made it legal, validated the husband-and-wife agreement.

"Cheap pens," Noreen said quietly to me. "Careful, don't get ink on my dress,"

Sheila cried and, wiping her eyes, said, "I'm so glad to see Noreen getting what she wants, what makes her happy."

"Like she doesn't always?" Ray glanced at her and smiled sideways.

"Good for you two," Del hugged us both. "I'm glad I was here to see it." He'd come right from work and wore his dark uniform. "Gotta get back to the garage," he said with a grin. "With you on your honeymoon, I'm short-handed for the next three days."

Reggie handed us a bottle of champagne with a pink ribbon tied around its neck.

"I know how you feel about this and it means a lot to me that you're here, Reggie," I told him quietly. I was a little choked up by the gesture.

"Bro, if this is what you pick, then I'm gonna back you up. Now let's get the party started."

Sheila's gift was dinner and she had made reservations at Alberto's, the nicest restaurant in town. Our little group drove to Fraser where we had a private room in the sedate, traditional establishment. Even though Sheila was hosting, Noreen had chosen Alberto's. She said it was a "nicer restaurant" because they had real silverware, and white linen tablecloths and napkins. Noreen was quick to identify nice things – she preferred them, sought them out.

After dinner, there was more laughing and talking as everybody hugged us, the bride and groom, and each other and slapped me on the back a few more times. Then, Noreen and I drove the short distance to the Gasthaus Eichler Hotel, one of Winter Park's finest, where we spent the night, our first night as a married couple. As I wrote *Mr. and Mrs. Kenneth D. Evans*, I felt the smile on my face spread through me. I knew, just knew this was the right thing, the thing that would unite us, bring a family close-up, make me feel part of what we would create. I was happy.

"Isn't this a lovely room? Hardwood floors with an oriental rug – what an elegant look." Noreen ran her hand over the polished wood of the antique dresser across from the bed. "And look at these sheets." Noreen fingered the top sheet on the king sized bed. "I bet they are 600 thread count. This is the kind of sheets we're going to have one day."

"Yeah, they're white, alright," I grinned at her. "That's all I know about them."

The next morning, we ate breakfast in the dining room. As we were seated, Noreen looked down at the highly polished silverware on the bright white tablecloth. She spread her linen napkin in her lap and smiled at the fresh bouquet of yellow zinnias and purple agastache in the clear crystal vase.

"Ken," she said to me, her husband of about 24 hours, "do you really want to wear a wedding ring? I mean, you work with car engines and greasy things, for heaven's sake. And it could be a safety risk. You might catch it on some random car part and hurt yourself. You'd be just as married if you didn't wear it." Her hair swung forward as she lowered her chin. She looked up, smiling at the waiter as he poured hot English breakfast tea into the delicate bone china cup. She looked at me like she expected an answer.

"What?" My coffee cup clanked into the saucer.

"Well, I was just thinking that if we return it, we'll have $127 to spend on something else." Her long neck and perfectly shaped head tilted and thick ash-brown hair fell to the left. Her warm eyes locked into mine. I looked down at the symbolic band and knew she had already made up her mind.

We returned the ring to the Wendy Funk's jewelry store in Winter Park on Monday morning. "Is anything wrong with the ring?" the clerk asked.

"No," replied Noreen, "we just changed our mind about it." She unfolded the receipt.

The clerk opened the cash drawer of the register, lifted the black clip and picked up $20 bills.

"You paid cash so I'll give you cash back."

"That's fine." Noreen edged me away from the spotless glass counter. "I handle the finances in our household," she told the young man in the dark suit.

Noreen lifted her right arm, palm up, to receive the money and the jewelry clerk counted the cash into her hand.

"Thank you." She folded the money, put it down deep into the black of her purse. She slipped her hand through my elbow and guided me out of the store in one almost fluid movement.

From the apartment she had shared with her brother, Noreen took only her clothes, shoes, makeup and a framed photo of her parents as she moved into the house Reggie and I had grown up in.

"It's fine, it's lovely," she said barely two weeks later. "But could we throw out this faded old rug and maybe paint the kitchen?"

"The rug was my mother's – maybe we could keep it? Sure, we can paint the kitchen. I'll do it. I don't want you around the fumes. You go pick out the color and I'll start Saturday morning while you're at Sheila's," I told her.

As soon as the ink dried on our wedding certificate, Noreen quit her job as dispatcher for the sheriff's office and began searching for a house. Every day, she drove around town looking for *For Sale* signs.

She asked at the City Market in Granby and the Pinewood Café in Frazer and The Lariat Diner in Grand Lake about someone who might be interested in selling a house. She drove to Winter Park to do our laundry at the Circle D Laundromat. She struck up conversations with cashiers, waitresses, anyone who would pass along local gossip and information about real estate. I thought it might just be a way for her to pass the time or an expression of the nesting instinct in a pregnant woman. But it was a serious pursuit for her and finally, with less than seven weeks to go before her due date, her chattiness paid off. She found the house she wanted.

"Kenny," she pleaded, "I love it. It's perfect for us. If you buy this house, I won't ask you for anything ever again – honest." Her head leaned to one side and her hair fell toward her shoulders. Her eyebrows tilted toward each other and her eyes seemed liquid with want. That night in bed, Noreen unbuttoned my pajama top, ran her hand over my chest, pulled me to her.

"Are you sure this is ok?"

"Mmhmm – we'll just be strategic," she said in a voice as smooth as close-cropped prairie grass.

Reggie and I had talked casually about someday selling the house where we had grown up. We met for dinner at Kate's. The discussion was serious.

"When Tooley died, I was really sad. I still miss her. But with her gone, I had to handle all the memories in that house." Reggie was quiet for a minute. "Before I moved out, I took an ax and chopped up Mama's dresser, the one where the fishhook necklace used to hang, and I threw the pieces into the fire." Reggie wiped his hands on the white paper napkin. "You knew that, right?"

"Yeah." My right wrist rotated so the bottom of the moist glass created empty circles on the tabletop. I looked at them like they were really important.

"I don't feel any real attachment to that house, even

though we grew up there. Now seems like the right time to sell it. MacKremmon is really growing and you shouldn't have any problem. Go for it, bro," Reggie agreed. I knew that Mrs. Brewster's son Aaron and his wife Holly wanted the house.

"My apartment's not much bigger than my pick-up but hell, I'm snug as a bug in a rug, as Mama used to say. I'm happy. Yeah, you just tell me where to sign." Reggie nodded, winked at the waitress and ordered another beer.

When all the paperwork was done and the house was sold, my half of the money made a deposit on the house Noreen had chosen. The monthly payment was more than I had wanted to spend but how could I say *no*? The house was a fresh start and I wanted that. I think we both wanted that. Houses were selling quickly – Reggie was right about MacKremmon's rapid growth. Quik Lube was expanding and I knew I had a future with the company.

Noreen and I bought the house from Mrs. Whitman who, at the age of ninety-one had been a widow for a long time and was leaving MacKremmon to move in with her daughter, over in Grand Junction. The daughter asked if we'd like Mrs. Whitman's overstuffed sofa and slightly scratched coffee table. We didn't have much furniture and I nodded but Noreen immediately said, "No, no thank you."

Mrs. Whitman owned the house outright and we had a good-sized down payment. Mr. Fullenwider was president of the bank in Winter Park and a loan was easily arranged; the closing process quick and simple. Still, my hand shook a little as I signed my name. Noreen's cheeks seemed even rosier than usual as she settled her shoulders, picked up the pen and wrote her name with a flourish. The house was barely outside MacKremmon, in a tiny hamlet called Azure.

Reggie borrowed a truck and he and Ray helped me move the basics – the double bed, a chest of drawers, a sofa and a couple of lamps – into the bungalow.

"Noreen, honey, where's the rug?" I had searched the truck twice.

"Oh, sweetie," Noreen walked over to me and put her arms around me, "I left it. It worked in that little house, don't you think? We'll get a new one – it'll make the living room look fresh." She tilted her head and gave me a little smile. I thought I saw victory in her batting eyelashes.

Ray and Sheila arrived the next afternoon. She brought three packages of diapers in newborn size and a beautiful handmade quilt in pale new-baby colors; she'd hand stitched the delicate yellow, green, blue and pink squares into place for her first grandchild.

She asked Reggie to go out to her car and bring in two heavy, flat boxes containing the pieces for a white crib and a matching changing table. Noreen looked at the boxes and would have jumped for joy but the weight of her belly kept her earthbound. Instead, she clapped her hands and grinned.

"Oh, Mother, it's the crib set I liked so much!" Noreen hugged Sheila. I recognized the set as the expensive one Noreen had said she wanted. I'd told her we couldn't afford it. Sheila's homemade quilt was laid aside.

"As my, uh, wedding present, I'm gonna help you paint the house," Ray told us. "Help you," he emphasized with a grin as we watched Noreen and Sheila opening boxes.

I looked at Reggie who replied with, "Yeah, I'm in. Who's buying the Coors?"

Reggie borrowed a power washer from the ski resort and got to our house Friday about two p.m. I took off early from Quik Lube and by dark, the sturdy house looked shaggy but spotless. Noreen had coffee brewing, orange juice poured and Sheila's homemade banana nut bread cut in slices when Reggie and Ray got there early Saturday morning. The three of us worked for two days, pausing only to eat. By the end of the day Sunday, bright white paint had the house looking as sharp as a new car just off the assembly line.

Ray was good at painting trim so the window frames and the front door were coated in periwinkle blue. At sunset, the three of us in paint-dotted fleece and jeans, stood in the middle of the quiet street. Each of us held a cold beer and surveyed his handiwork.

Reggie had his arm around my shoulder and he grinned. "Here you are, bro, the homestead for the brand new Evans family." I nodded, felt almost embarrassed with happiness. The three of us clinked our beer cans.

Painting the nursery was a job I wanted to do by myself. The following weekend, I rolled on the pale yellow color Noreen had chosen for the walls. Using some of the same fabric she'd put in the quilt, Sheila made curtains with little animals on them for the window. Reggie showed up with a six-pack and he and I sat in the floor with a screwdriver. The two of us put the crib pieces and the changing table slabs together. When Noreen and Sheila walked into the room, it was ready. Pride, excitement, happiness – they were like pistons pumping in my chest. I watched Noreen fold her hands over her beach-ball abdomen and survey the room; I thought she must be happy, too.

When we were mostly settled in the house, Noreen and I strolled around the quiet streets of the hamlet every night after dinner. With only days to go, Noreen was puffy with baby and a name for the child filled the bubble of conversation.

"What do you think, Ken? Your name means 'handsome' and we want to choose a meaningful name for our baby."

"Well, my mom's name was Edith." I knew it was a risk but I suggested it anyway. As I said it, I looked down and kicked a clod of dirt. Noreen stopped still in the middle of the street. She took her hands out of her jacket pocket and put them on her hips as she turned to face me.

"Name her after your mother? The one who left you? No, huh-uh, I don't think so." I felt almost physically hot in the cool air, but her reaction was not totally unexpected. We walked another full block in silence and then Noreen said she'd always disliked her own name.

"Have you ever heard of anybody who's ever done anything being named *Noreen*? No, and you never will," her mouth soured at the corners. "I hated my mom for naming me that."

"Your mother did the best she could, Noreen. I guess all parents do."

"Well, I'm here to see to it that our child, our daughter, has a name with panache and élan, a name that will convey confidence and get her somewhere in life. I'm thinking of Lavinia."

"Lavinia?"

"Well, it's a beautiful name that means 'daughter of kings.' It has a certain ring to it, don't you think?"

"And if it's a boy?"

"Well, we'll think of something. But he won't be Ken, Junior," Noreen was firm, "or Chester." She sighed and rolled her eyes.

Chapter Eleven

Noreen's labor seemed long and I stayed with her, held her hand even though she went through alternate spells of yelling at me, screaming for me to get away from her, and squeezing my hands and sweatily thanking me for being there.

Migod, I thought, *how does a woman do that?* Even though we'd driven to Winter Park and attended six weeks of childbirth classes and Noreen's doctor reassured me that things were going along normally, there were times I thought my wife might die, wondered that a woman going through that kind of twisting pain didn't.

When Lavinia was born, she produced a faint little puppy-like wail and as she was put in my arms, I felt my mind and body jellify. Was it relief or did I fall into the abyss the moment of Lavinia's birth? I wasn't sure – it didn't matter.

I felt a strangeness, an odd diagonal feeling, at sensing a part of all humanity here in this perfectly formed infant. How could I, a man who felt lopsided, like he was living in angled pieces that somehow didn't always fit together, find those parts snuggling into each other to make up a smooth whole? I wanted to contribute the part of myself that would grow up straight, become a person and then a singular individual, a particular complete human entity and I would work to do that.

I often heard other parents say things like, "We're so in love with our baby!" and I wished I could separate my feelings from my very being, peel the spiritual layers of love from my physical existence, long enough to examine them in that way. My love for this tiny, wrinkled thing named Lavinia was instant, internal, flowed from a primordial spring somewhere inside me, flowed like a powerful spigot had been turned on, flowed freely and without my control or actual involvement in it. It was just suddenly there, washing through me, permeating my cells, carrying me along, and it gushed like clear mountain spring water gurgling over smooth rocks.

I often held Lavinia and just stared into her green eyes. I nuzzled her powdery-smelling head and frequently wondered how it was possible for a parent to leave a child, to unlove one, detach from it, abandon an offspring like it was a worn out, used-up truck. Even though Noreen wanted me to put her down while she was still awake, I regularly rocked Lavinia until black eyelashes drooped into sleep.

"You'll spoil her," Noreen said often. The words were foreigners who could find no way into the homeland of my mind. I was enveloped, not just wrapped up but sunk, like a man in a bog. Love for this baby soaked into me like water soaks though a wool coat thrown into the lake. And I thrived on it. At work, the garage mechanics would tease me about the "goofy smile" on my face when I talked about her – and when I didn't. I didn't care. Lavinia was a beautiful, healthy baby and I was a goner and I knew it. Noreen insisted that I call her Lavinia but it just never seemed right. When it was just the two of us, I called our daughter Liv.

When Liv was sixteen months old, Del officially retired and I was named manager of the shop in Lyons as well as the MacKremmon Quik Lube. Ray got promoted and moved to Colorado Springs where he helped open a new Quik Lube shop, five minutes from the US Air Force Academy.

Ray and Noreen had grown up in a cozy little house just off State Road 13 in Meeker, the county seat for Rio Blanco County. The town, famous for hosting Billy the Kid and President Theodore Roosevelt, was named for US Agent Nathan C. Meeker who was killed in 1870 by the Northern Ute. Now Meeker was known as a stable agricultural community with a backbone-of-America population.

Once Noreen and I were settled into the house, Noreen wanted her mother to be closer, more available. Sheila quit her job at the quilt shop, left Meeker, and accepted Noreen's offer to pay part of the rent on the apartment she and Ray had vacated. When the baby arrived, Sheila took care of Lavinia three days a week while Noreen completed a course in bookkeeping at the community college in Steamboat Springs.

Late one afternoon, I came home early. I could hear Noreen and her mother talking as they sat on the floor of our little house.

"Thanks for doing this, Mother," Noreen was saying as they watched baby Lavinia go sleepily back and forth in a musical, mechanized swing. "I feel like I have to work. Ken just doesn't make enough money."

"Honey," Sheila said, "Ken is a fine man. He's a good choice and I'm sure he's doing his best to make you and the baby comfortable and secure."

"Well, maybe. But if he had gotten more education or had a government job, he might be a better provider for us."

"Well, you know I'm happy to be with Lavinia while you take your classes. When she naps, I sit down with my quilting."

I coughed and slammed the back door. Sheila got up

and gave me a hug. Noreen spoke but she didn't take her eyes off Lavinia.

A week later, I had spent the day at the shop in Granby where the front office had reopened after being renovated. Quik Lube wanted all the front offices to look exactly alike. I had worn a white shirt and tie for the official ribbon cutting and the photo would be in Thursday's paper. It was a good day and I was feeling as satisfied as I was tired. I got home late and the baby was already down for the night.

I put my hand on the knob of the partially open door to her room and smiled as I looked in at her sleeping in the crib. My shoulders relaxed – I could almost feel my Quik Lube cares slip off of them. Then I walked into the bedroom where Noreen was propped up in bed. She had a book in front of her and the bedside light on.

"Still up? What are you reading?" I stood still and stared. "Eh, your hair. It, uh, looks different, shorter."

"Oh, yeah. While Mother was with Lavinia, I got it cut today at La Chic in Winter Park. It's called a pixie cut - like it?" Noreen turned her head from side to side.

"Uh, sure. You, uh, look just fine." It was gone, the thick undergrowth a man's fingers could struggle through; the deep fleece of hair that held warmth and invited intimacy, cut away, discarded, swept up off the floor, tossed into the trash.

"With a three month old to take care of, I thought it would be more convenient this way. It won't take long to wash and dry." Noreen tilted her head so I could see her profile and gave me a flat-lined, level-highway smile. She reached over and switched out the light. She snuggled into her side of the bed, facing the wall. As I lifted the sheet and go into bed, I felt cold, the cold that emphasizes loss.

I always loved the woods, the way they looked and the way they smelled, and by the time warm summer arrived, I put Liv in a backpack harness so we could hike. I talked to her constantly and told her everything.

"These are called great quaking aspen, Liv," I would tell her, "can you hear them clattering in the wind?" Or I would say, "Listen, do you hear the birds? The sparrows say 'tweet, tweet.' And that blue one is a scrub jay. He'll peck a cat, my mama always said." I wanted to tell her everything, to point out every nook and cranny of the world and the stars to her.

By the time she was 22 months old, Liv knew each animal by the call it made. When we heard a "woo woo," she would immediately say, "Ah-well." She recognized pictures of sheep with a "baa-baa" and she watched me feed fish in a nearby stream and puffed out her cheeks imitating them with, "Bloop, bloop." She knew milk came from cows we saw in the fields and she loved to feed the chickens at Mrs. Fullenweider's house. She called out "ribbit-ribbit" to frogs and did a funny, stiff-legged hop every time we spotted a rabbit.

Before the girl walked, Noreen was negotiating with her.

"Let me put this pink bow in your hair and I'll put lipstick on you," she would say. The head shaking would stop while the toddler considered the bright red temptation. Then she would slowly nod her head up and down and Noreen would smile. Noreen always knew what appealed to Lavinia and she didn't mind pulling that very thing into the situation, coloring the picture with the most appealing crayon, holding up the winning card; it almost always worked.

At least once a week, our little family went hiking. As we tromped through the woods together, we would often stop. I would squat down so Liv could carefully examine a leaf or a flower.

"The bees like the blossoms on spirea," I told the little girl. "They get nectar and then they fly away, back to the hive and make honey from it. We'll stop at Hafeli's on the way home and get some honey." Liv soaked up everything she heard and her vocabulary branched out like a young pine in sunshine.

I had always liked to camp and Liv enjoyed it, too – Noreen went with us three times and we had a lot of fun. But the fourth time, it was late October and many of the woods animals were getting ready to hibernate.

The three of us were in the tent, Liv asleep, warm between Noreen and me on the air mattress. I think we were dozing when suddenly, there was a scratching on the wooden picnic table outside. Then, in the bright light of a full autumn moon, we saw a shadow of a black bear. She stood up tall on her haunches and moaned. She looked like a skyscraper tilting over. Her front paws hit the ground with a thud and she lumbered over to the tent. She rubbed her back against the strong front tent stake. I put a finger to my lips. Noreen and I were both shaking as we grabbed each other and held tight. We froze. Only our eyes moved and we looked at each other and at Liv. I know both our brains were racing, trying to figure out what to do, how we would get out of there if we had to. Suddenly, the bear, for whatever reason, gave a loud grunt and lumbered off.

"Ooohh, Kenny, I was so scared!" Noreen's arms around me tightened. For a second we trembled and hugged each other close. We both forgot Liv was asleep between us until she said, "Eh, eh, eh" and flailed her arms around. We looked down and Noreen and I panted hard and looked at each other for a long second. Then she pushed me away, checked to be sure Liv was asleep. My wife scooted back to her side of the air mattress, rolled over and pulled up the blanket.

About dawn, we broke camp. Noreen never said anything but I felt like that would be our last camping trip as a family. I was right. She told everyone she missed the remote controlled TV so she could be in charge of the action. She never went with us again.

But Liv and I continued to camp by ourselves. Frequently, we pitched our tent near a stream. Liv loved to finger the smooth rocks near the water whether it was a trickle or rushing stream.

"Basalt," I would say, "is a dark, iron-rich volcanic rock. You can find it throughout Colorado and it comes from lava flows thousands of years ago. There's lots of it up in Flat Tops."

Or she might pick up a pebble of sandstone, granite or marble. "Marble from Colorado was used in the Lincoln Memorial in Washington, DC," I would tell her. "That's a long way away but you'll go there one day."

The girl brought each rock and geode home and kept the collection in a clear acrylic shoebox, shrine-like, in her room. I'd see her sitting in a little white chair at a little white table, spending happy hours counting and examining, almost adoring, each one in turn.

Camp-outs require a campfire and we always built one so we could cook over an open flame. My favorite photo, the one I kept on my dresser for years, was of our daughter sitting cross-legged, holding a stick poking straight out over the fire. Through puffs of smoke, four-and-a-half year old Liv sat smiling at the gooey, marshmallowy mess on the end. A little pile of rocks was nestled at her right hip.

Chapter Twelve

Soon Quik Lube went nationwide, opening shops in most of the southwest states. MacKremmon was growing and more residents meant more cars, cars that needed service. My success was growing right along with the company's. My photo had appeared in the local edition of the *Rocky Mountain News* when I was named manager of two more regional stores. My paycheck had increased, a reflection of long hours spent at the shops and the additional responsibility I took on. With her accounting certificate, Noreen got the job handling the books for the MacKremmon and Lyons shops, both of which I managed. I tried to chalk it up to being at work a lot, but I felt Noreen stiffening a little, changing, and my stomach knotted up sometimes when she spoke to me.

I had heard Noreen and Liv's loud voices aimed at each other one night as I opened the front door. They both stopped when they saw me, they each looked kind of guilty, but it was obvious they were arguing about something they didn't want to tell me about. I never found out what it was but I tried to ease some of the mother-daughter tension by getting home to dinner a couple of nights a week.

One night, I was later getting home from Quik Lube than I had wanted to be. I snubbed out my cigarette in the car's ashtray as I pulled into the driveway. Noreen and Liv had finished eating dinner. Their plates were on the kitchen counter and Liv sat in her chair. Noreen was just closing the freezer door and she turned toward me with a carton of vanilla ice cream in her hand.

"Dad," Liv said, "you're just in time for dessert." She smiled at me.

"Great." I turned on the water in the sink and rubbed the bar of soap between my palms. "What's for dessert?" I rinsed my hands.

"Peach cobbler and ice cream," Noreen told me. She was holding the carton down on the counter with her left hand and her right elbow went up, almost airborne, as she shoved the big spoon into the frozen whiteness.

I turned off the water and snapped a paper towel off the roll.

"No, thanks," I said without looking at either of them. "Can't do it."

I tossed the wet, wadded towel onto the countertop and pulled the ever-present package of cigarettes out of my shirt pocket. My mother's face was in my mind as I shook one out, put it between my lips and flinted the lighter into flame. As the tobacco caught fire, I walked out the back door and closed it behind me. The grey-white smoke joined the night clouds as I looked upward.

Some months later, I went home one night to find that Noreen had cut up two of Lavinia's favorite t-shirts, hacked them to shreds with scissors.

"I never liked those t-shirts. They sent the wrong message," Noreen had answered when I asked her about it.

I had no idea what words and images were on the shirts so I couldn't quite understand Noreen's anger. But work took up most of my thoughts so I left it alone.

Then, about six months later, on the day my corporate office supervisor visited, Noreen called.

"What's wrong, Noreen?" She almost never called me at work. "Is Liv sick?"

"I'm going to call the sheriff. Lavinia doesn't want to go to tap dance class so she's hidden my car keys. I won't put up with this kind of behavior. I just want you to know I'm calling Travis."

"Noreen, honey, Livie is eleven years old. I can't come home right now so put her on the phone. I'll talk to her."

"No," there was a gritty sound in Noreen's voice, "I'm calling Travis to come over here. Maybe it'll put some fear and respect into Lavinia. And I've told you a thousand times, don't call her *Livie*. It sounds like some mangy, stray dog." She slammed the phone down in my ear.

It wasn't just incidents involving Lavinia that seemed strange to me. One rare rainy fall morning, I rolled over in bed and felt cool air coming from the empty space next to me. Even though we hadn't made love in months - Noreen always said she was too tired after working and taking care of a child - her absence created a lack of warmth, a coolness in our bed and I noticed. The clock showed 3:45 a.m. when I got up and slap-footed my way into the kitchen. I was drinking orange juice from a Pep Boys coffee mug when Noreen came in from the garage. As she shook raindrops off her trench coat, I noticed that under it she was wearing a sheer pale mint-green nightgown. I'd never seen it before. The skin near my eyebrows bunched together and I felt my eyes narrow.

"Noreen, it's four in the morning and you've been out – and you're wearing your nightgown? What's up?"

"It's raining. I decided to drive the car around in it. Poor car was dirty and hadn't been washed in weeks. The rain cleaned it off. C'mon. Let's go back to bed."

I set the mug down on the counter and followed her like an obedient sleep walker.

By the next morning, I was willing to believe that maybe I'd dreamed the whole thing; it was too odd to have been real. But then I got to work and Abner, who changed oil on Bay #1, got my attention with a question.

"Hey, was that Noreen with the sheriff out on Old Silt Road early this morning? I was helping Johnny deliver newspapers about three o'clock and I thought I saw their cars parked next to each other. 'Course, it was raining and I couldn't see so good." Abner looked down at the tire gauge he was twisting. I could tell that he was trying to sound off-handed about it.

"Oh, yeah," I replied, equally casually, "she said she drove the car around so it could get washed in the rain. I guess Travis was checking on her."

That night at home, I asked Noreen about it and she said, "Yes, I was out on Old Silt Road. I guess I drove a little farther than I planned to. Travis was out patrolling, there are always more accidents when it rains. He just wanted to be sure I was ok and you should be grateful. Besides, the car got a good wash so what are you complaining about?"

"Old Silt Road is a long way away. I'm not sure this makes a lot of sense." I looked down as I scratched my head.

"A lot of things don't, Ken. If you want things to fit neatly into your life, do the crossword puzzle." Noreen slammed the closet door shut. "And tell Abner to mind his own business." She walked out into the hall as I climbed into bed by myself. I tossed and turned and finally got to sleep but something about the incident bothered me, kept gnawing at me like an invisible pest.

Liv was twelve, talking about being thirteen, when Quik Lube told me they were sending me to training in the new reporting system. Along with nine other managers,

I would spend three days at the company's training site in Atlanta, learning the ropes and getting comfortable with the new Point of Service computer program.

"Maybe while I'm there, I'll take a few days drive down to southern Georgia, try to find my mother or some of her people," I said to Noreen one night as we finished dinner. I looked down as if I was talking to the plates with their scattered dabs of mashed potatoes and brown left-behind flakes of meatloaf. I picked up the plates, one in each hand, and carried them to the counter.

"What? *Pour quoi*? Do you know where she was from? Do you know who her people are? Where will you look?" I knew she wanted concrete answers.

"Well, she always talked about peaches and she used to say she was from peanut country so I thought I'd start looking in Plains and Americus. Reggie remembers a few names she used to mention and I'll write some letters before I go. Maybe I'll get some answers or maybe I can locate some official records," I replied. "She drove off in Dad's car and it was never found. Maybe there's some kind of record of the license plate with the State Patrol. There must be something."

"Well, I just don't see the point of it," Noreen was piling the dishes into the sudsy sink water. She scowled. "I bet Jimmy Carter is the only famous person from those podunk towns. Besides, it seems to me that one of two things will happen." She faced me, folded her arms in front of her and leaned back on the counter.

"One, you won't find anything. Do you even know her real name? Didn't your dad always say that Dawson was either a name she made up or she was married before?"

I looked down at the two iced empty glasses, rounded slivers of ice and a flat slice of lemon in the bottom of each, as my hands slid them onto the kitchen counter. My eyes moved on a runny little splotch of salad dressing, about to drip over the edge of one of the plates. I stood very still as if by doing so I could make everything, including Noreen's objections, freeze.

"And two, even if you do somehow miraculously find out something about her, don't you think it will be a big disappointment? I mean, she's probably dead by now. You know you've built her up in your mind as this beautiful Southern belle – which I have to say, she obviously was not. I mean, she smoked like a chimney, didn't she? And from the stories told around town, she had a hot-blooded personality and no taste in clothes. And she was overweight and out of shape, right?

"The reality of it is that no flesh and blood person is ever as lovely and perfect as the image you have of her. You know your imagination has had years to recreate her and who she really is or was, is just not going to live up to that." Noreen pulled yellow rubber gloves over her hands and they disappeared into the kitchen sink.

"And then, even if you do find her, or any of her kin, they won't be what you think they are. They might all be trailer trash. You always said her grandfather had a still – maybe they're all falling-down drunks or deadbeats or something. You'd really be let down, Ken, you know you would." She looked over her shoulder at me as she turned to the sink. Her right gloved hand lifted a clean plate up and onto the wooden drying rack on the counter.

"Then you'll come home all disappointed and *triste* and I'll be the one who lives with you in that mood. I don't want you moping around, making Lavinia and me depressed with your disappointment. Besides, we can't have Lavinia being related to some band of southern hicks. She has a place in MacKremmon society and I'm going to make sure it's not besmirched by some country bumpkin backwater relatives. I think you should leave well enough alone."

"Yeah, well, you could be right," I said. "But she's my

mother, Noreen. If it was Sheila, you might think different about it." I knew I sounded defensive I just couldn't help it.

Noreen yanked off the gloves and smacked them against the rounded white edge of the sink.

"How typical of you to have such a self-centered attitude. You'd think you'd give more thought to Lavinia and me and how all this might affect us." Her hands were firm on her hips and as her head rose regally, her hair flipped angrily to the side.

I lifted the package of cigarettes out of my shirt pocket and headed for the back door. I lit a cigarette as I walked into the dark of our back yard. I inhaled, tossed the used-up, black-headed match into the Scotch broom by the fence post. I exhaled a thin ring of smoke that spiraled upward and dissipated instantly. I pulled the back gate closed behind me.

Chapter Thirteen

I OVERHEARD HOURS OF CONVERSATIONS between Liv and her friends that focused on how much they were looking forward to officially being teenagers, what they planned as celebration, how the new milestone would impact their lives. The girls in her class, and especially the ones in her snug little circle, were all attractive but Lavinia stood out. She was tall, slim, poised and one of the boys had said her green eyes were "bright gherkins surrounded by Maybelline." Her skin was as clear and flawless and bright as Colorado's 350 days of sunshine.

She could have been a junior beauty queen had Noreen not felt beauty pageants were tawdry, showy and tackier than a cheap politician with dyed hair. Birthday parties had replaced camp-outs because Noreen thought the sun might provoke freckles on those beautiful cheekbones. Noreen had plans. She chose her daughter's activities and friends as carefully as she chose the expensive clothes.

She would tell her, "Lavinia, you can't go to Annie Showhalter's in just any old outfit. If you get a good grade on your spelling test, I'll order a Jimmy Buffet shirt for you to wear to her birthday party – it's Hawaiian themed, right? You have to look nice but not splashy. Your family's been in this area a long time and Annie's mother is an *arriviste*." Annie's dad, the current mayor, had gone to UC-Berkeley and married a woman from Oregon. That was fifteen years ago but as far as Noreen was concerned, the woman was new to town.

"Ken has to work so Travis is going to pick you up. You'll get to ride to Annie's in the squad car. Won't that be fun? All the other girls will be *jaloux*."

Once a week, Noreen dropped by the two shops where she kept the books. The office was tiny and I understand there was always good-natured elbow-dueling and jostling for space.

"Here, I'll get it. You go on back out there and do the heavy, manly work," she'd say to the mechanics as she eased them away from the cash register. She knew that kind of bantering made the customers relax and laugh. Sometimes, they were having car maintenance work done during their lunch hour and they appreciated the staff being time sensitive. When she was in a good mood, she used her warm smile and direct eye-contact to make friends for the shops.

MacKremmon sent its town trucks and snowplows to Quick Lube but Travis' deputy Duane explained to me that the sheriff's department had a long-standing contract with Shealy's Garage in Fraser and they would continue to send their cars there.

"I guess that's only fair," I replied. MacKremmon had nearly 2,500 residents and some families had two cars or a car and a pick-up. Even without the squad cars, business was good at the shop.

The Town of Lyons ran all the city trucks through Quik Lube and so did other local businesses like John's Wells and Loukonen Rock. The Lyons shop always seemed to be busy on Thursdays, and while I was in MacKremmon, Noreen dropped in and spent several hours. When the mid-day rush began to tamper off, usually by 4 p.m., Noreen headed home where she had a desk made out of two saw horses and a flush door and that's where she did the actual bookkeeping.

A new subdivision, Richmoor, was being built on the edge of town and Noreen had been talking for weeks about the houses where all the kitchens had microwave ovens and dishwashers and workspace islands. She could have a proper home office, maybe even get a desk.

"I shouldn't have to work at all," she said one night after Liv had gone to bed. "But since I do, I think I should get to decide where we live."

"I guess I don't have any problem with that," I told her. I swallowed hard but put some energy into sounding like I was completely onboard. "It's obvious Liv needs more closet space. Why don't you talk to a real estate agent about a house?"

Noreen flashed a smile, touched my cheek and that night before we got into bed, she slid her hands up under my t-shirt. I put both hands into her thick, heavy hair. It had been awhile.

Two days later, a realtor from Grand Lake took us through the model home. Her high heels clicked on the hardwood floors and our voices echoed through the hollow-sounding rooms. She held a clipboard in the crook of her left arm and used her right hand to gesture. "Lots of natural light, huge closets, the best dishwasher in its price range."

Twenty days later, we signed the papers and were handed the keys. I felt strong and straight-up as our little family prepared to move into the third shell-of-a-house completed in Richmoor. What would become the lawn was still mud and Reggie backed the rented truck into the new driveway just off the freshly paved street. The county had built a spacious new recreation center a few blocks over and now that we were within walking distance, Noreen signed Lavinia up for French classes and swimming lessons.

The day after we moved in, I cited unpacking as my

excuse to leave work early. I stopped at Kate's and got a banana split to go.

"Daddy, you know I can't eat that," Livie straightened her back and looked away not letting her glance linger on the moist, tempting carton. "There must be a million calories in that thing. Mom would have a fit."

"Alright," I chuckled and put the cold fruit jumble in the freezer. "Let me help you with that box." I loosened the laces, took off my steel-toed work shoes and set them neatly by the door. My socked feet padded across the hardwood floor and I sat down next to Liv. Ragged piles of family photos had pushed the lid off the rectangular box like they were angry, revolting against being ignored for so long.

"Look at this one," Liv held up a photo of the three of us. She was about four months old, I was holding her, staring at her. Noreen stood looking at the camera, a pleased look of "I did this," on her face.

"You were a beautiful baby, Livie." I reached into the box.

"Hey," she dug down into the heap, "here's one of you with Uncle Reggie. He looks like he's just heard a good joke. You were a handsome little boy, Dad, but you look so intense."

"Yeah, Reggie's got on what Mama used to call his permanent grin but I was always more serious. Daddy's cousin Cal took that photo. Our mother had been gone about two weeks when Cal came to stay for nearly a month. My dad needed the support – geeze, that must have been a tough time for him."

I felt my lips mash together and my eyes blur as they riveted onto the photo.

"Too bad about your mom leaving."

"Yeah."

"I guess it's one of those deep hidden family mysteries. Every family has 'em, don't they?"

"Uh, yeah." My shoulders squirmed as if in an effort to escape. Neither of us spoke and in just a few seconds, my mind flashed years. Then I cleared my throat, lifted my chin and looked at my daughter.

"I always thought I might find my mother someday." I coughed.

Liv nodded softly and didn't speak. She held the photo of Ken and Reggie in her left hand and ran her right index finger around the edge. Then she held the aging photo with both hands and brought it close to her face for just a moment.

She laid the black and white photo gently down on top of the others in the box.

Chapter Fourteen

Five days after we moved in, boxes were still whompy-stacked in the craterlike living room of the house with the brand-new smell. It was a Saturday morning and Liv had just come home from French lessons.

"*Bonjour*," she threw her monogrammed canvas tote down in the foyer and walked in to help me as I stood ankle deep in wrinkled newspaper.

"You look pitiful, Dad," she chuckled lightly. "Let me help." For nearly an hour, we talked and laughed and pulled paper and bubble wrap off Noreen's valuable knick-knacks.

"Liv, I've mentioned to you that I have to go east, to Georgia, for some company training." I looked down at the Swarovski crystal Eiffel Tower in my hands. "I'm going to try to find my mother while I'm in that area. I'd like it if you'd go with me." I looked at her and forced my voice to lower at the end of the sentence; forced it to have the sound of definite.

"Go with you? I can't miss school, Dad, and I have lessons."

"I know you have a lot of activities but you've quit swimming lessons, right? And spring break is coming up.

You'll be out of school for a week and your French lessons will take a break, too. It'll take us two and a half days to drive to Georgia. I've written to some places and I have a couple of possibly useful replies. I think we can follow-up in a couple of days. Then I'll put you on a plane back to Stapleton airport and your mom can pick you up. I'll go on to Atlanta and drive home when the training is done."

"Hhmmm. Mom would not go for that idea."

"No, I expect she won't. But you'd get to see some of the country. And we'd get a chance to spend some time together, just the two of us."

"Well, I don't know … I'd need some new clothes …"

Noreen yoo-hooed her way in the front door and dropped two brown sacks of groceries. "A little help here," she insisted.

"Can we talk about this some more later?" Liv hadn't said *no.* I nodded.

I waited until we'd eaten a frozen pizza and salad dinner, and Liv asked to be excused to go upstairs to her room.

"Go," I told her. "Those boxes of shoes and scarves and hair bands won't unpack themselves." I leaned forward in my chair as I watched her climb to the second floor of the house.

"Liv and I unpacked some of the living room stuff this morning," I told Noreen as I lifted my glass of iced tea.

"Mmmm …"

"Yeah, and I talked to her about going east with me. We'll drive to Georgia together and spend some time looking up my mother. Then I'll put her on a plane home and I'll go on to the company training." I looked down into the glass.

"What the hell are you talking about?" Her head snapped up suddenly attentive and her voice was husky, low in her throat. "No, you are damn sure not taking Lavinia with you. I won't allow it. She is not going to get mixed up in this."

"'Get mixed up?' Noreen, she is my daughter and she

and my mother are important in my life. We'll get to spend some time together, get to know each other better. I think it would be great for the two of us. I've talked to her about it and I think she's interested. I'm sorry you don't think it's a good idea but you've got some time to think about it."

Noreen grabbed my plate and slapped it onto the brand-new hardwood floor.

"No way in hell," she said before the sound of china splintering had died.

I flinched when the plate shattered but I knew what I wanted to say.

"You always say you do what's right for Liv – and this is right for her. Calm down, Noreen, and think about it. It'll give Liv a chance to see more of the world than just MacKremmon. This isn't about you. Don't think it is and don't make a selfish decision."

Noreen did not reply and her jaw remained gritted together the rest of the evening.

"It might be good for her to see the country." Sheila told me later she had advocated for the trip when Noreen talked to her about it.

"I don't want her to go, Mother. Can't you understand that?" Noreen had crossed her arms in front of her and clamped her jaw tight. Sheila said her look was piercing.

"Think of it this way," Sheila told me she had soothed Noreen – after years of practice, she knew how. "You'll have nearly a week by yourself. You can read, watch TV, see and do whatever you please. No schedule and no fixing dinner every night. You'd be on your own."

I watched Noreen chew her lip for three days and finally one morning at breakfast, I heard her say, "Lavinia, do you want to go to Denver Saturday and shop? You'll need some new clothes for your trip."

Liv packed two suitcases for the trip. Her return airline

ticket was bought and Sheila had given her a blank journal to serve as a log for the trip. Noreen hugged the girl tight and looking over her head, gave me a look that would ice over an igloo.

"You be sure to call me, *mon cherie.* Make it collect – I'll pay for it. I want to hear your voice every evening and know you're ok."

"I'll miss you, Mom. You'll be all right?"

"Don't worry about me. I can think of creative ways to spend my time while you're gone. It's you I'm concerned about."

"She'll be ok, Noreen, stop worrying. This is an adventure and she'll have something to tell her friends about. That new Nikon you bought her is perfect for the trip." Noreen turned her head and my kiss landed somewhere near her earlobe. I made a show of very carefully placing Liv's suitcases in the trunk before I slammed it shut.

"Buckle up, Liv."

She waved out the window as we backed out the driveway and headed down the empty street. I beeped the horn and it echoed through the beginnings of three new houses, dull piles of light sand and a white bathtub surrounded by stacks of pristine wallboard.

Chapter Fifteen

We pulled into the Holiday Inn just off Interstate 70 in Hayes, Kansas, after six and a half hours of steady driving. We registered at the motel, took our bags in and turned on the air conditioning to freshen up the inside of the standard room. Then we asked at the desk about a local place to eat. The young man in the white knit shirt with the green emblem pointed and we walked to the Chuckwagon Grill. We ordered chicken fried steak, mashed potatoes and salad. Knowing I didn't have to drive any more that night, I had a beer.

"Well, kiddo, what do you think so far?" I tipped the shapely glass and tasted the cold liquid.

"Well, after we left Denver, the scenery's been a little boring. But it's fun, Daddy. I had no idea Colorado had so much open space and so many miles of railroad track. Kansas already looks different. What are we gonna see tomorrow?"

"Miles and miles of miles and miles," I told her with a smile. The waitress had a tattoo on the inside of her right arm and it showed below the sleeve of the uniform shirt. She slid full plates in front of us. She sat the ketchup bottle down and I noticed she had a small grimy ring on each of her eight fingers.

A skull with shiny red eyes glared from her middle finger. Her fingernails looked grungy and I was glad Noreen couldn't see them.

"So things are ok at school?" I looked at Liv as my knife and fork worked together to cut into the steak.

"Yeah," she replied without looking up. "Things are fine. Why do you ask?"

"Well, I know your mom gives you a lot of … shall we say guidance about your friends and your clothes and everything. I'm just wondering if you're ok with that." A piece of steak went into my mouth and I chewed and chewed.

"Oh, it's no problem," Liv held her back straight and her chin angled. "The first time I heard the word 'manipulate' was in American Government class. Mr. Harvey was talking about how wealthy donors get politicians to do things for them. I knew right away what it meant. I've got Mom figured out. I usually know what she wants and I manage to use that to get what I want. I don't leave a lot to chance when it comes to her. I know what she's like." She looked at me with a gaze as level, open and firm as the country highway. She tapped the white mound with her fork, as if she were royalty knighting the mashed potatoes.

"Sounds a little judgmental." I took a sip of beer and glanced at a Roy Rogers poster on the wall.

"It is judgmental. I've got an opinion about everything. Mostly, I know what I want and I'm pretty firm about getting it. Maybe I've just learned the lessons well. Whatever." She gave an unconcerned shrug.

To change the subject, Liv sang along with Michael Bolton as *How Am I Supposed to Live Without You?* played on the jukebox. She passed on dessert and I ordered bread pudding knowing she would eat a few bites of it.

Liv was teaching me some French words as we strolled back to the motel. I struggled with pronunciation and as she laughed, her hands lifting in the air, her hair swinging loose. A white car swerved, screeched, lurched, leaned hard into her. She tilted, fell, crushing and scattering pebbles under her body. A whoosh not a thud and she was on the ground. Livie screamed. It was slow motion in my head but it had all happened fast. The car had careened sideways then skidded away leaving Livie lying on the curb and me bending over her.

The local sheriff had been drinking coffee at the counter when the waitress heard the commotion and shouted at him. He grabbed his hat off the adjacent stool and rushed to us. He knelt down to look at Liv as he asked, "Did you see who it was?" I shook my head and felt for broken bones in Liv's arms and legs. From the cruiser, he radioed the information on the car to the deputy and eased the black and white up next to my hurt girl.

The sheriff and I each lifted an arm and put it around our shoulders. As gently as we could, we helped a shaking, sobbing Liv into the police car. I sat in the backseat and Liv sat sideways, legs up on the seat, leaning back against me. The shock of it all left my heart beating so hard my shirt moved in and out. My mind couldn't help me with words to say so I kept repeating, "You'll be ok. You'll be ok."

The cruiser's siren blared and the red light flashed for the five blocks to the local emergency room, a tiny corner in a small local hospital. The doctor later told us he was from Chicago, serving his time in a rural community as partial payment for his student loans.

"It's her ankle." He was brusque and to the point. "We need to get her cleaned up."

A nurse had given the girl a local anesthetic and the doctor used sterile tweezers to pick rocky bits of asphalt from her leg. Each piece made a *plink* as it landed in the curved metal bowl. It was a deep, long scrape and Liv bit her lower lip and whimpered. Black dust and tears mixed on her face and her hands twisted the corner of the lightweight cotton blanket the nurse had wrapped around her shoulders but she never cried out.

"I think it's shattered probably from being slammed against the uneven edge of the road. It's gonna need surgery." He put ointment and thick gauze bandaging over the ugly new wounds. "We can do it in the morning."

"No, no, not here." Liv shook all over and she held an ice pack to her left shoulder. Her upper lip was cut and the jagged scrape had begun to swell. "I wanna go home." She was in charge, even in pain and shock, even with her nose runny, she knew what she wanted. "Dad, I want to go home. You need to take me home. Get me home." The look she gave me was controlled and rigid, an order not a supplication. "And look at this, my new blouse is ruined."

"Can I drive her back to MacKremmon?" I asked the physician. I pulled the hospital blanket up over the torn blouse. "Would she be ok?"

Liv was loaded into the backseat of the car, ice packs on five different spots and blankets tucked around her. I got two black coffees from the vending machine in the hall. The middle-of-the night phone conversation with Noreen had not gone well.

"Hmm ... hello?" When she answered, I thought I heard a muffled voice.

"Noreen, it's me." As soon as Noreen heard my voice, a sharpness bit its way into the conversation. I told her what happened.

"You idiot!" she screamed, "this is all your fault, Ken! I told you not to take her with you on this harebrained trip! Ohmigod, now look what's happened. You get her back here as soon as you humanly can, do you hear me? I don't care what you have to do. If she wants to come back, you get her here!"

Noreen said she was going to call Doc Hedstrum who

would call MacKremmon Medical Center and alert them to get ready for the injured girl. Later Sheila told me that Travis had driven Noreen to the hospital. He wasn't in uniform but the night desk nurse recognized him and she glanced quickly from his face to Noreen's as she handed over three pages of forms and a pen.

As I drove through the dark, Liv lay in the back, in a netherworld state, a result of the pain medications. She whimpered occasionally but insisted she was fine when I stopped at a garishly lit truck stop where I filled up with gas, used the restroom and bought bottled water. The road was good to us and except for big trucks, there was very little middle-of-the-night traffic. In a little more than five hours, I pulled the over-heating car up to the new MacKremmon Medical Center which had been built when the town's population reached 5,000.

The automatic doors opened as Noreen rushed out, followed by the doctor on duty and an orderly with a gurney; Travis stayed just inside the doors. During the commotion of comforting Liv and moving her, I glanced at Travis and gave him a slight nod. Noreen did not once look at me.

The sky went from hazy pink to feathery blue as the diagnosis was made. Liv's ankle was indeed shattered and in need of surgery. A specialist from Denver was called. He would be there by eleven in the morning. Liv was given a mild sedative. Travis and Noreen had come to the hospital together in her car so he called his deputy to pick him up. Noreen refused the waiting room and sat next to the bed. The orderly handed her a pillow to soften the hard grey metal of the standard-issue visitor's chair.

Part of the hospital's usual process was the blood draw that had been done immediately when Liv was admitted. About 10 a.m., a technician clad in green scrubs came in with the full lab report. By then, I was standing next to my wife in the clean sterile room. Noreen asked the tech if we could see the results.

I felt my eyes snap with surprise when I saw Liv's blood type. I knew immediately that should our daughter need blood, I would not be able to donate. I was not a match. It shouldn't have come as a surprise to me – and yet it did. Noreen and I had kept the secret about her biological father for a long time. I knew the time had come – we had to tell her. About 11:30, when they wheeled a woozy Liv into the operating room, I went outside for a cigarette. I rubbed my wrist and paced.

"It took a little longer than we thought," the surgeon told us nearly three hours later as he untied his cotton cap and peeled it off his head. "We put in two pins. But the surgery went well. Ankles can take a long time to heal and she'll have to take it easy for awhile. She'll need therapy after the swelling goes down. But she's young and we don't expect any problems. The therapy is important and I'll write the orders for it."

Noreen and I shook his hand and thanked him. And after the doctor went through the door marked Lounge, Noreen turned to me.

"Goddamnit, this is all your fault." The words came out hard, rapid. "You stupid, low-rent grease monkey. You had to take her with you, didn't you? And then you let her walk on the streetside when any gentleman with good manners would have made her walk on the curbside. You didn't get the license plate of the car that hit her. You were in some dump of a town that barely had medical care. And you did all of this because looking for your long lost mother trumps your concern for this child." She paused to take a breath. "I just hope you're happy."

"Don't be ridiculous. Of course I'm not happy about it. I love Livie and I feel awful about all of it. But what's done is done. Take a deep breath, Noreen. We need to pull together. We'll get through this."

"Get through this? Is that what you think? She's in pain, she's in shock, she's just come out of surgery and all you can say is, 'we'll get through this'. And did it ever occur to you that I might have had plans while you were away? You've ruined more than just Lavinia's week." Noreen slammed a thick lock of hair into place behind her left ear.

"Look, Noreen, I know you're angry but calm down." For several long seconds, neither of us spoke. Then I said, "I think we need to talk to Liv. I think this is the time, the time to uh, to tell her …" I couldn't finish the sentence.

"What? Are you insane? She's hurt, she's unsure of what's going to happen next and you want to tell her *now*?"

I felt my eyes move from Noreen's face to my wrist and then to the floor. I barely nodded. "We ought to talk to her before someone here in the hospital says something. Yeah, I think we should. If we don't do it now, we'll have to do it at some point. This may not be the perfect time but yeah, I think now's the time."

"No, absolutely not. There is no way. You haven't wanted to do it before and you're not going to do it now. I won't have it, do you understand?"

For almost a full minute, beeping machinery, carts clacking down the hall and the soft footsteps of professional caregivers were the only sounds. Noreen was standing in front of me and she twisted her hands, bit her lips, and scratched her fingers through her hair as if she might find some reply there.

"I don't want to do this, Ken. This is a terrible time to tell her. Why, oh, why haven't we told her before?" Finally, Noreen sighed and her head leaned downward as if in defeat.

"It may be a terrible time but there's never going to be a good one, is there? You can see this hospital is a busy place and someone is going to say something about the blood types. Liv's smart and she'd figure it out and I don't want it to happen that way – we don't want it to happen that way. We need to tell her. And we need to do it together and we need to do it now." I had been pacing and stopped in front of Noreen. I stared at her. The minute seemed as long as the linoleum hallway.

"I guess you're right." Noreen sighed deeply and her shoulders sagged. "We need to be the ones to do it and we need to tell her. You're right - someone could say something."

She crossed her arms but did not look up. "All right, we'll tell her. But not right now. When she's heard the results of the surgery, maybe then she can stand to hear *verite feminine*."

"The what?"

"The truth, Ken."

"Yeah, ok. I need to think about what to say. I think we should do this as a family but I'll … I'll tell her."

I went home and called the corporate office to tell them what had happened, that I would go to the next training session. I showered and slept for a few hours; fitful, guilt-ridden sleep. I felt terrible about the accident but it was just that – an accident. And I knew what came next, what had to be done. Noreen had said she was going to call Travis and then doze on the worn nubby waiting room couch. I expect that she shifted and twitched, too, knowing that telling the truth was a fact, prickly and real as barbed wire, that lay ahead.

Noreen told me later that she was there when Liv came out of recovery and was wheeled still groggy to her room. Noreen said she watched the nurse adjust the IV, check Liv's pulse and make notes on the chart.

Anxiety showed in Noreen's shoulders as she hunched over the hospital bed and looked into her daughter's face. Liv's eyes fluttered open and she blinked slowly, blinked with questions, blinked with uncertainty, blinked without full understanding.

"It's ok, sweetie," Noreen told the girl whose eyes focused on her mother's face. "The surgeon told us the operation went fine."

Color was coming back into Liv's cheeks and she wanted to be reassured.

"Yes, he says you'll need therapy but everything looks good." Noreen smoothed her daughter's hair back from her forehead. They exchanged one little smile. Then Liv's look changed to one of concern.

"Oh, Mom, I'm so sorry. I was wearing one of my new outfits and it's ruined." By tomorrow, Liv might feel some pain but for now the strong meds were in charge. Her mind had the freedom to think about clothes.

"Don't worry about it. Ken will buy you new clothes. You just focus on getting well and don't think about anything else, ok? I'm right here. Do you want some water?"

"Yeah, just a sip. I'm going back to sleep. Why don't you go home and take a shower? And bring me back something to wear. I must look awful in this hospital gown. I don't want anybody to see me like this."

Noreen said Liv had smiled a little and when her daughter's head had eased its way back so sleep could take over, she sat for awhile before she did indeed go home. I heard the shower and was vaguely aware that, hair still wet, she took a blanket and a pillow to the living room couch and slept a few hours there.

My wife and I arrived in the kitchen at the same time.

"I'll make the coffee," I offered. "And we can drive to the hospital together."

"It's the least you can do," she snapped. "And just so you know, I don't think I'll ever be able to forgive you."

Noreen and I walked into Liv's hospital room together. Noreen pulled the metal chair up next to the bed and sat down. I stood and I could feel my knees wobbling. I dragged the pale blue curtain around us and spoke first. I wasn't sure what words I used even though I'd practiced a speech most of the night. Noreen never took her eyes off Liv; didn't even nod or acknowledge me in any way as I spoke.

I had expected Liv to scream, yell, throw things – I was prepared to see her act out the shock. But instead an ugly, bleak silence hovered. The three of us were secluded in the fabric cocoon, Liv propped on several strict white pillows on the hospital bed, with Noreen and me next to her.

Our daughter stared without blinking at us, the couple she thought of as parents, while I spoke in haltingly phrases and groups of words. Her back got rigid, I thought, and for a split second, when the actual words took meaningful shape in the air, a look of shocked surprise registered on her face. I wondered if she might cry or shout. But Liv seemed to almost instantly be composed, rigidly in control. For a full minute, only the tiny beep of machinery sounded in the snug space.

"Get out."

The flat-line tone in Liv's voice caused Noreen and me to, simultaneously, take in a surprised gasp.

"Lavinia, don't worry about it. How 'bout next week, we'll go to the shelter and get you a kitten. You'd like that, wouldn't you?" Noreen leaned toward her and extended what she knew was an appealing offer. "You can think of a good name for it. And it'll give you something soft and fuzzy to cuddle and you won't have to think about all this."

"Just get out."

For a second, everything stood still. Then I pulled the curtain a few inches aside and Noreen walked out into the hall while I stood half in, half outside the wavy barrier. I chewed the inside of my jaw like I was trying to remember the words to a song; I wanted a cigarette so badly. I stood and waited for the long part of a moment. I looked at Liv, steeped in pale and unyielding anger, surrounded by cold monitors that blinked in colors. I stepped my entire body back in and pulled the curtain. I sat in the stiff-backed metal chair Noreen had vacated.

"Livie, your mom and I, well, we always meant to tell you. We tried a couple of times but we, I, uh, we just couldn't seem to do it. You're our daughter and we love you, your mom and I both do. That's what counts, isn't it? We're your parents and we're here for you."

I reached for the hand lying on the spotless white sheet. But before I could touch it, Liv snatched it away and folded both arms across her chest. She looked down, her eyes focused on a spot on the sheet. She refused to look at me, to bend or flex to the news in any way.

I tried to explain that I had always been hesitant to tell her the truth but it didn't matter because somehow, in my bones, in the weightlessness that made up my very cells, I was her dad and I didn't care, had never cared, who the biological father was.

"The right moment for that talk just never happened," I told her honestly. Now the words had an almost artificial feel in my mouth, as if I had manufactured them to talk to her, had created and shaped each syllable in an effort to explain the facts, was using them to patch up the puncture and regain the closeness we once had.

"I know this is a tough time for you to find this out. You're a teenager and your life is changing. You're going from girl to woman and you're trying to figure things out. I'm so sorry this came out now and I know you're hurt and upset and confused." I rubbed my left wrist. My eyes never left Liv's.

"It may take some time but this is not going to change how we feel about each other. You still have the same love, the same home and the same peace of mind you had before the accident. I know you'll think about all this and when you want to talk, you just let us know, ok? I'll be right here where I've always been."

I had hoped to see the girl nod, acquiesce to reason, soften to the words. But she didn't. Her jaw remained tightly controlled and she barely blinked. My ears throbbed with the beat of my heart and the need for a cigarette gnawed at me. I knew she needed time. My mind couldn't help flashing back to when my own mother left and how there were too many chaotic thoughts in my head; it took time before I could funnel them into a single-file line.

I stood up, and felt Liv stiffen as I leaned over and kissed her on the forehead. I pulled back the soft fabric barrier and walked to Noreen, standing with arms folded across her chest. Together we emerged into the cold efficiency of the hospital corridor.

"She knows I'm here for her, we're here for her," I told my wife, "that's what counts now." I tried to hug Noreen but she stood straight and hard, arms rigid at her side, head stiff on a firm neck and eyes straight ahead. "Let's give her some time." When my arms fell back to my sides, she soundlessly turned and walked away.

The hospital kept Liv another twenty-four hours and Noreen stayed with her. With her mother toting prescriptions and care instructions, Liv, shaky on crutches, hobbled through the door at home just after noon the next day. Noreen had put a clean sheet over the expensive new chair and matching ottoman in the family room and Liv sat in it, leg propped up and chin held high. She reminded me of an old person who has to look through the bottom part of the bifocals, the part with the greatest magnification, as she looked down on me. I hoped I looked bigger, magnified, dad-size to her.

Liv was still stung and angry and I felt I had some making up to do. Every morning, I would leave a note for her to find.

"Liv," it might say, "see you tonight and we'll finish that jigsaw puzzle." Or, "Am bringing red velvet cupcakes from that new shop on Youngfield Avenue for dessert tonight, Liv, be hungry!" I made her laugh as I read the newspaper's comic strips with character voices – the scratchy way I did Snoopy in *Peanuts* was her favorite.

The swelling began to subside. After three weeks, the specialist came from Denver and examined the ankle carefully.

"Looks like the swelling has gone down. Let's get therapy started. In some cases like this, participating in therapy often makes the difference between complete healing and a permanent limp." All three of us thanked him.

Liv went to therapy on Mondays in Fraser, Noreen drove her. She said a young therapist with the straight hair and dark blue scrubs put the girl through strenuous exercises. I came home early on Tuesdays to help with her with the exercises she'd learned the previous day. Every now and then, I could feel her green eyes on me and I thought the gaze was softening her view of me, easing her acceptance of me, deepening our closeness. It seemed we were patching up the puncture between us, slowly ratcheting back up the magic hydraulic lift of closeness and warmth that I felt had been at its lowest.

Chapter Sixteen

Liv didn't like physical therapy, complained it hurt too much and she either avoided it or did a minimum number of the prescribed routines. She began to favor her left leg so the pressure was never completely on the repaired ankle even though the doctor had said it was ok, the bone and muscle needed the stress to re-form and heal properly. I watched Noreen giving in too easily to the girl, letting her slack off the maneuvers that would strengthen the joint. I knew that speaking up about it would only anger Noreen and make Liv cry.

Finally, after five months, the capable young physical therapist told Noreen she had done all she could. Liv had a slight limp. The therapist said that in her experience, Liv probably wouldn't make any more progress and the insurance was going to stop paying. Noreen argued and made several phone calls. The discussions were loud but in the end, Liv was discharged.

In the nearly ten months that had passed, Noreen had taken Liv shopping in Denver twice; they bought new jeans, slacks and stylish boots to hide the scars around the joint on her lower leg. Even with a new wardrobe, Liv was self-conscious about the limp and she preferred staying home after school rather than hanging out at the rec center. Daily the large house bubbled with Livie's friends, none prettier or more expensively dressed than she was. Teenage fragrances of popcorn, nail polish and hair spray escaped whenever I opened the front door.

The last of the April snows were seriously considering May thaw when, in a move that shocked all of us employees, Quik Lube was sold to a big conglomerate, headquartered in Chicago. For the next six months, the new parent company audited the books and the procedures, analyzed expenditures and manpower, compiled the data and made some decisions.

Then it cited the country's overall financial lull and specifically, lack of expected profit growth in my shops. Six shops were closed in Colorado, including three of the four that I managed.

"Your shops always seem to be busy," the regional manager nervously adjusted his necktie as he explained to me, "but our reports show that the profit in your shops has remained nearly static and other shops show financial growth. It's not optimum operational strategy and as part of the company's efforts to remain financially viable, we're releasing these properties."

"You're closing my shops? Is that right?"

"It's nothing personal, Ken, it's a business decision." His mouth was a straight line. I wondered if he had real lips or just that string in his lower face.

He told me they were sending in one of their corporate guys to manage the remaining shop, the one in MacKremmon, and they gave me sixty days notice. Noreen was furious.

"How can you do this to Lavinia? First, you drag her off from home on some stupid road trip. Then you let her get hit in a terrible accident and she has a permanent disfigurement because of you. Then, she finds out you're not her real father and now she'll have to give up her activities because there is no money. This is a delicate age for a girl, Ken, and look what you've done." Noreen's words spattered like mud flung up onto a windshield. "And you realize I'm now out of job, too, right? I just hope we'll still be able to afford cat food." The bedroom door slammed and now I was sleeping on the couch.

I had no answers. I felt like embarrassment showed in my every movement. The last two weeks at Quik Lube were like walking through vats of old motor sludge for me. One part-time and three full-time technicians were losing their jobs and I just couldn't look them in the eye. They were all young men with families and while two had found work nearby, two others moved out of the area. As each technician left, I shook his hand and thanked him. It took all my strength.

For a full week after I left Quik Lube, I got up early every day, grabbed my backpack, made a thermos of coffee and went to walk in the woods. The quiet, the shelter of the overhead branches, the peaceful lack of accusations and glaring looks were like salve on a burn. I absorbed nature's quiet, the healing majesty of the views, differing only in the color of leaves. The peaks looked like they were drawn on the edges of my walks and I thought of them as gathering, protective enclosures around me. I clutched the scent of the wild like a comforting coat. Now I knew exactly what my mother meant by those words.

Dinners at home were quiet with Noreen talking only to Liv. Clothes, manicures and school were the topics and when they started speaking French to each other, I carried my plate to the counter and walked to Kate's for a couple of beers.

Eight days after my last day at Quik Lube, I got a part-time job at the gas station out on Route 81. I'd known Ross Black, the station owner, for years.

"It's not much of a job for a guy like you," Ross told me with a shrug.

"It's a big help, Ross. Thanks for taking me on. Maybe the locals will get the word I'm here and come by to have some work done."

"Well, I always welcome new business." Ross grinned and shook my hand.

To avoid going home and facing Noreen, I began to spend my time off hitting the local bars with Reggie.

"Man, where you been?" Reggie asked me one night. We were in Tabernash at the Buffalo Rose leaning with our arms on the bar, hands around thick glasses of local brew. A group of young men in carefully molded cowboy hats and shirts with silver-studded front pockets flaps was on-stage, mangling country and western tunes. Several couples were Texas two-stepping around the scratched up dance floor. Peanut shells crunched underfoot.

"We coulda been having this much fun all along but, noooo, you had to be a family man. I told you, didn't I? Didn't I tell you? Look what we've missed." Reggie clapped me on the back and burped.

I lit a cigarette, looked down at my third beer and nodded. I had missed Reggie but Noreen had always thought Reggie was "coarse" and she only let me invite him to the house on Christmas day.

"Yeah, I've missed you, too, bro," I said to my only sibling. And I meant it.

"Rosie," Reggie bellowed at the pretty barmaid whose name was Barbara, "another round for my brother and me."

It got to be a habit, a routine for us to go home before dawn, noisy-drunk and either fake-happy singing or depressed and sloppy maudlin. Reggie would crash at the house, sprawled and smelly on the living room sofa. Many nights, I was too drunk to make it up the stairs and I'd be the arms and legs

Liv saw sticking out of the expensive chair when she came downstairs in the morning.

"Phew, Dad and Uncle Reggie stink," I heard Liv tell Noreen one morning. The nights were turning toward windy fall chill and windows had been closed to keep it out. Liv held her nose, pinched it against the sour odor of clothes sweaty with heavy male body odor and the yeasty mash smell of beer.

"I hope the place airs out before my friends get here at six." Three gold bracelets clanked together as the girl waved her hands to help clear the air.

That night, Noreen confronted me and said she couldn't stand the drinking.

"What will the neighbors think? You know this is a nice neighborhood. Nobody in Richmoor wants their family exposed to rowdy drunks," Noreen said. "Wednesday when I got up, you'd left the front door open – not unlocked, Ken, but open. Anybody could have walked in. We could have been robbed or killed." Her eye lids lowered slightly. "And you both smoke. You might burn down the house with Lavinia and me in it. I don't like it, I don't like it at all."

I nodded. But nothing changed. The following Thursday, late in the afternoon, my head was pulsing at the same rate as the gas pump feeding high test into Mrs. Adams' Oldsmobile. Ross came out and took the pump handle out of my hand.

"You got a call."

"Daddy," Liv's voice sounded firm as brushed steel, "Mom's packing our suitcases. She's says we're going to stay with Grandma."

"I'll be right there," I slammed down the phone and lit a cigarette as I got into the car. I threw up my hand in a solid wave and saw Ross frown and nod.

"Noreen," I called as I opened the front door, "what are you doing?" I sniffed the house's still-new aroma and took the stairs two at a time. Noreen was in our bedroom, standing next to the queen size bed. Expensive sheets peeked out from under a thick down comforter. Huge decorator pillows sat regally plumped against an upholstered headboard.

"I'm leaving, Ken," she said, not even looking at me. "And I'm not sneaking off in the middle of the night. I'm leaving now, in broad daylight. Your mother didn't have the courage to do it this way, but I do." My eyes followed my wife as she moved around the room. I wanted a cigarette.

"Look, just stop, stop for a minute. Let's talk about this, ok? I know things have been tough for the last twelve months or so but this is just garden-variety unhappiness. Every couple goes through it."

I spread out my workman's hands, glanced at them, quickly fisted them up and stuffed them in my pants pockets. I had to be careful not to touch anything and run the risk of getting motor oil and gasoline fumes on what I thought of as Noreen's nice things. I glanced at Noreen to see if she had noticed I'd walked across the carpet wearing my work shoes or how the sharp oily-smell on me contrasted with the sweet, powdery fragrance of the room. There I was, the garage worker, feeling painfully inferior to the atmosphere I lived in with my wife. The clash was a terrible thing to feel.

"I want this marriage to work. We both want Liv to have two parents, I know we do. Isn't there something we can do? Some kind of marriage counseling we can go to?" I rubbed the spot on my left wrist that seemed to burn, the old charred flesh hot anew.

"No." Price tags dangled from three Brighton belts and two Dooney & Burke handbags she slapped into a suitcase. "If I wanted to go to counseling, I would have done it. I'm not going to counseling with you," Noreen looked at me for the first time, "not now, not ever. So don't bother me with it again." Noreen stood with her hands on her hips, her hair was still as summer grass and her eyes focused on me.

"Besides, some psychiatrist would have a field day with you. You think you can be all nice and giving and win a woman's love and approval and that'll make up for your mother dumping you. Well, it won't and no matter how you reach and yearn, you'll never get enough, never make it up, never feel satisfied in that department."

I coughed as if it could smother the comment. "This isn't over," I told her.

"Yes, Ken, it is." Noreen zipped the suitcase shut. She stood up straight and folded her arms across her chest. No hope showed in the eyes that stared at me.

I reached into my shirt pocket for the package of cigarettes as my heavy footsteps took me downstairs and outside. I lit up. I blew the smoke out from pursed lips, emptied my lungs, and felt my chest and my will crease, fold in like a deflating, flatening inner tube. I needed a drink.

Sheila, always frugal, had lived quietly for several years Noreen and Ray's old apartment. Noreen knew her mother would give in to the request that she and Lavinia move in with her. And she did.

I took flowers to Noreen the following week and when Sheila opened the door, I could see that homemade quilts on the twin beds in the guestroom had been replaced by expensive throw pillows and coordinating spreads. The closet overflowed and an overstuffed red shoe bag hung over the door. Sweaters and purses were piled like an earthmover had lifted them up onto the closet shelf. Dozens of lipstick tubes tumbled over each other. Pots of lotions and half-squashed tubes of cream sat without lids and crowds of perfume bottles elbowed each other for space on the vanity's top.

Once a day for three months, I walked to the telephone booth at the edge of the gas station's lot. I dropped in a coin and lit a cigarette while I waited for Sheila's answering machine to pick up. Every time, I left a message for Noreen to call me. She never did. And when I went to pick up Liv so we could get a hamburger together, Noreen was always out.

Soon, Noreen hired Nick Tompkins, the sharpest divorce attorney in three counties. Through him, she cited irreconcilable differences and filed for divorce. It all happened fast. The house in Richmoor went up for sale and an excited young family bought it within forty-eight hours.

Noreen stored some of the furnishings and took some of the most expensive pieces to a high-end consignment shop in Steamboat Springs. They sold to second-home owners in no time. She boxed up my clothes and dropped both cartons at the gas station.

In little more than a year, everything I thought I had worked for, lived for, was like a grease stain fading on the pavement – gone from the distinct, arched colors of the rainbow to runny, messy rivulets where the hues all merged to form bottom brown.

I tried to make Noreen happy, give her everything she wanted. I had sent her flowers and left messages. I didn't want to give up but what did I have to offer her? Having a husband who pumped gas was not in Noreen's plan.

Sheriff Travis Nolen's wife, who had suffered with multiple sclerosis, died and it seemed like all of MacKremmon turned out for the funeral. Six weeks after our divorce was final, Noreen married Travis. He sold the house he'd shared with his wife and Travis. Noreen and Liv moved into a gingerbread-trimmed house listed on the Historic Register, located in the prestigious center of town.

Liv told me that the county employee health plan allowed for plastic surgery and even though she still limped, the scars from the accident disappeared, were erased, as if the formation of the new family folded up, enveloped them and created a smooth, new facade.

Until now, Liv and I had worked out our time together. But once Noreen was married, she sued for sole custody of the girl. A court date was set and the judge, a hunting buddy of Travis's, awarded it to her and gave me parental visitation rights - Wednesday evenings and all day Saturdays.

Noreen said Liv complained that I showed up staggering, smelling like stale cigarettes and cheap bourbon too many times. Within a year, we were back in court. I protested it wasn't true, that I couldn't afford to drink bourbon. But the judge honored Noreen's request and restricted my visits to once a month and half-day on holidays only. I felt my head sag toward my chest as I left the courtroom. I headed to the nearest bar. I stayed until the barmaid repeatedly reminded me of closing time.

Liv and I kept to the official visitation schedule. One Wednesday evening three months later, we ordered pizza at Woody's. A bleach-blonde young waiter with six studs took our order and Liv brought up the subject I knew she had been thinking about for years.

She slid her water glass gently back and forth on the slick tabletop, "I talked to Grandma."

I didn't have to ask about the subject of that talk; I knew.

"And?" I clamped my hands tightly in my lap, nicotine stained fingers intertwined and strained against each other, hidden under the table, out of Liv's sight.

"Well, I wanted to know if she knew that you are, you know, not my biological father." She pulled the clear plastic straw out of the glass and chewed on it.

There was a pause and I looked down and noticed that one prong of the cheap metal fork was bent. It seemed to point accusingly upwards toward me. My hands twisted against each other.

"You've always had a close, loving relationship with Sheila," I said.

"Yeah, I felt – well, not comfortable but not *un*comfortable talking to her about it." Liv blinked a glance up at me. She picked up the saltshaker, stared at it and set it back down. "I was curious and scared to talk about it. But curious won out."

"And did talking about it help?" I looked into Liv's green eyes, my hands still in their out-of-sight location.

"Well, it did. I asked her if she knew all along and she said, 'yes.' But you know Grandma. She said she respected what you and Mom wanted so she never offered to talk about it. She said she always thought that one day, I'd ask her and she would tell me the truth."

I stiffened a millimeter, involuntarily leaned toward Liv and awaited her reply.

"She said Mom never confided in her about who my biological father is. Did she ever tell you?" She put the straw back into the glass and took a long sip of water. "Did you ever even ask?"

I thought the last five words had sharp edges.

"No," I told her honestly, defenselessly, "I never asked. I always thought that if your mother wanted me to know, she would tell me. And then, you were growing up and well, truthfully, our family ran as smoothly as a V-8 engine on high-test. We were enjoying life together and your biological parentage was a fact I almost never thought about it.

"I've always been open with you that my mother left me, Liv, so I know what it's like to be abandoned. I know the sense of self-blame, the feelings of inferiority, the lack of inner stamina I felt. I could never do that to you, could never leave you. I just knew I'd always be there for you. I have always loved you." My hands came up to the tabletop. They ached from being clenched together.

"Yeah, well, Mom says that if it weren't for you, I wouldn't have had the accident that left me with a limp." The server set down a large Coke. "She said that when you lost your job at Quik Lube, you suggested I get a part-time job or babysit for pocket money."

"Yeah, I did. I thought ..."

"Well, I am not going to babysit and I'm not going to work. I want to have fun while I'm in school and you and Mom can figure out a way to make that happen for me. I kind of think you owe me." There was a wintry chill as she spoke.

"Well, I've always felt like your father," I tried to warm up the conversation.

"But we don't look alike."

"No, I guess we don't." I sighed and sat back in the chair. "But you love the woods like I do," I told her. Liv smiled just a little and blinked.

"Yeah, I used to. We always had a good time camping out. I still have that box of pretty rocks we collected."

The waiter slid a pepperoni pizza onto the middle of the table and Liv reached for a stiff paper napkin and wiped our conversation clean.

The following month, I watched Liv gliding on the ice at the rink in Winter Park. Later, I noticed the expensive skates slung over her shoulder as she walked ahead of me to a table on the deck. The weather was cool but still pleasant enough to sit outside for a bite to eat before I took her home.

I'd hoped we'd watch the sunset together. Pale blue was broken by fluffy white coming through the fabric of the sky and we saw horizontal stripes of pale salmon. But a large white delivery truck blocked the waning of the day. The sun was setting behind it, beating on the side of the refrigerated vehicle. I couldn't help but think that at the end of the twenty-four hour spin of the earth, the sun was probably making the contents inside uncomfortably hot.

Liv ordered a cup of hot cocoa and a grilled cheese sandwich with fruit as a side.

"You know," she bit off a corner of the greasy orange and brown triangle, "Travis wants to adopt me legally and he'd like it if I call him 'Dad.'" Her eyes looked straight into mine while she chewed.

"And how do you feel about that?" I asked.

Liv shrugged and swallowed. "Well, that way, we would all have the same last name, like a real family. I've thought about it and I think I'm ok with it. I'll be Lavinia Nolen. It seems to work out – for me. What do you think?" Her green eyes glanced down at her plate and she picked up a slice of dill pickle.

"I noticed your new skates. Paramount, right? Did your mom give them to you so you'd talk to me about this?"

Liv nodded. "Yeah, I really wanted them. Paramount is the best, some Olympic champions wear them. They're beauties, aren't they? Besides, she says the whole name thing is no big deal."

"Is she right?"

"Well, yeah, I guess she's right. There are lots of feelings involved, don't you think?" She bit off the pointed end of the pickle with a snap.

"Mmmm. And my feeling is I'd hate that. I always wanted to be your dad, do the things dads do …"

"And you were great," Liv didn't let me finish. "You were. Really. But this way, I'll have the same last name as Mom and Travis. We'd sound like a family – which we are."

"Livie, I'll just tell you. I don't like it. I feel like your mom has always been able to sweeten any deal by offering you what you want. This time is no different. I did my best to be a good parent – and a good husband. It wasn't my idea to give up on all that. But – well – sometimes things happen." I paused and heard my own thumping heartbeat. I physically craved a cigarette.

"You know this will mean an end to our time together, there'll probably be no more evenings like this. Once all this is legalized and you are officially Travis's daughter, I'll have no parental claim, no legal right to you and your time." There was a hammering sound in my ears.

"The skates fit?" I took a sip of water and saw Liv nod. "It sounds like you and your mom – and Travis, too, I guess – have talked about this. I personally don't think it's fair of your mom to put you in this spot. She should have talked to me about it."

Liv said nothing but she stopped eating and folded her hands in her lap. She sat stiffly patient in the chair and looked hard at me.

"If that's what you want and you've thought about what it means, I guess I can live with it." The desire to put my fist through a wall seemed almost palpable. "But I don't like it." I paused and looked out at the kids on the ice. "What do you want to call me now?"

"Mom says I could just call you 'Ken' - would that be ok?" She picked up the Coke and put the straw to her lips. Her eyes never left my face.

I nodded slowly.

Liv gave a little shrug. "I think that could work. You've always been good to me – and to Mom - but you're not my real dad and you've always known that." She looked at me and I felt goose bumps go down my arms. "Now that *I* know it, I think calling you by your first name is perfectly fine with me." She looked at me and her chin lifted.

"Yeah, ok," My throat was suddenly dry, parched, a forsaken desert. "It wouldn't be my first choice, none of this would be, but I guess that'll work." The moisture that should have been in my throat seemed to have moved up to my eyes.

I dropped Liv off, went home and drank a six pack of

Coors before sleep forced its way between my thoughts.

In a little less than a year, Lavinia Nolen walked smiling across the stage to receive her high school diploma. She still had a slight limp but the scars at her ankle were gone and she wore a dress, not slacks, under her graduation gown.

In honor of graduation, Noreen and Travis held a reception at the Grand Elk Country Club where they were active members. I was invited and went just long enough to hug her and say, "Liv, I'm so proud of you."

The champagne toast was too much temptation and I stood, ready to leave, when I heard the beginning of Travis' speech.

"As Lavinia's parents, let me say how much her accomplishments mean to Noreen and me."

Chapter Seventeen

NOREEN HAD ALWAYS TALKED about seeing Liv go away to school, to a prestigious college, a prominent girls' school, maybe even an Ivy League university, definitely somewhere out of state. But no matter how hard she pushed it, the eighteen-year-old maintained control; Liv held tight to her own choices.

"Travis will buy you a new car, a convertible, a red one if you want, when you go away to school. If you choose to go to school locally, well, a used one is the best we will do," Noreen told her with a shrug.

"I limp when I walk, Mom. I don't like meeting new people because they always think I'm a gimp. Do you think there's any way in the world I would go off to one of those snooty schools where everybody comes from uptight, perfectly formed families? Can you imagine I'd want to see the looks of pity on people's faces?"

"I do hear what you're saying but it's a little limp, Lavinia. New friends might be too busy looking at your beautiful face and elegant clothes to notice. You could give it a chance."

"No way. I'm staying right here in this area where

people know me and no one will stare or make fun of me."

Enrolling at the community college in Glenwood Springs was a way to assert her independence while minimizing exposure to new people, and that's what Liv chose. She did well in all her classes, especially chemistry. That's where she met Brian.

Brian Nelson Harkness was tall, slim and broad shouldered. Noreen said he had an oval face and long, thin nose that seemed to say "patrician old family" to her. Dark hair and deep brown eyes behind dark framed glasses added to his handsome appearance and he had quiet, genteel manners. He was a graduate of the University of Colorado in Boulder and working as a chemistry teaching assistant while he finished graduate school.

Brian's father, Dr. Theodore Nelson Harkness, descended from a family of Scottish landowners. The oldest son had married an Englishwoman, a direct descendant of Admiral Horatio Nelson, the third earl of Newton, England. The family had come to Virginia in the late 1770's and, within a decade, owned a cotton plantation. After the Civil War, two of the brothers had migrated west.

Dr. Harkness had held a PhD from the Colorado School of Mines in Golden where he spent his academic career as a well-respected, well-loved professor. Along with three colleagues, Dr. Harkness had developed an approach and a checklist for cleaning up after certain laboratory spills. It brought recognition from environmental and academic groups and a little money to the four professors. Three years ago, Dr. Harkness died of a rare form of skin cancer.

Brian and his mother Claire, who now taught senior English at Fraser High, had moved to the area. Possibly due to his height of more than six feet, Brian had developed a habit of dipping his chin and leaning into each conversation. Noreen gushed that she found it endearing.

"Well," Noreen told me, "most of the girls in this town think they've moved up the social ladder if they marry somebody from Aspen or Steamboat Springs. I always knew Lavinia could do better than that. Brian is educated and his family line goes back a long way. Did I tell you he's a direct descent of Admiral Nelson of Great Britain?"

About a hundred times, I nodded.

"And Travis' mother was a MacKremmon so Lavinia's children will have quite a pedigree." Noreen had a smile on her face that chilled anyone who might think of arguing. "Brian's handsome and I think he's more than acceptable. I guess he won't make a lot of money teaching but at least she's not marrying somebody with grease under his fingernails."

I swallowed and pretended to ignore the insult. "As long as he's good to Liv, he's okay in my book. I just hope he takes the commitment seriously and never hurts her."

Noreen's shoulders sagged and she crumpled up one side of her mouth. "Take a look at your life, Ken. I'd say you're hardly in a position to judge anyone." She turned and walked to her new SUV.

"And stop calling her *Liv*."

I believed Liv and I were becoming close again. One balmy spring night when the snow was changing from mush to gone, we met at The Library in Frasier. I knew when Liv called, that there was a point to the meal. It was a Wednesday evening and the restaurant was not crowded. The dark wood of the walls and tables, the polished brass around the bar and the thick, eavesdropping fern in the hanging baskets all added to the quiet, refined atmosphere.

We each ordered and when the waitress walked away from our table, I silently lifted first the knife and then the fork. I looked at each utensil carefully and didn't speak – I waited for Liv to drive the conversation. I looked at her steadily while she talked about new clothes she and Noreen had bought on a recent shopping trip to Denver. I wanted a cigarette but nobody smoked in a restaurant anymore so I focused on straightening the silverware to take my mind off of it. I sipped my water. Liv chose the moment the waitress set our plates down in front of us to tell me she planned to marry Brian.

"Ken," she explained carefully, "you know you're important to me." She paused for just a second and patted my wrist. "And I want you at the wedding, Brian and I both do. But Mom says that it's appropriate for Dad … eh, Travis to walk me down the aisle. She says he really wants to. She says it's what everyone expects. And besides, all the etiquette books say it's the proper thing to do." She picked up her steak knife and focused on the plate as if thoughts of the wedding had drowned in the brown juice of the slab.

"And he's taller than you are. I can lean on his arm to walk. That way, I won't be some limp-along in a white dress going up the aisle." Liv was cutting her steak as she glanced up and saw me lower my head and wince.

"And she's promised you the expensive designer wedding gown you want if you go along with that, right?"

Liv nodded and I felt my chin sink to my chest. I knew what was going on and once my appetite recognized it, thoughts of food walked abruptly out on me.

Liv and Brian's wedding was a big social deal and everybody in MacKremmon and the little towns close by attended. Liv's bridal photo in the newspaper took up three fourths of the page in the *Style* section.

I had funds from the sale of the house in Richmoor and while I had spent some money drinking with Reggie, I wanted Liv to have most of it. For the last few years, I had lived about five miles out of town in a rented trailer, an old doublewide with a built-in bed and plenty of loose-doored cabinets. The mobile home's dim-white sides were scratched up with years of hard wear.

Reggie often came out to check on his pot plants behind the trailer. When he first saw the trailer, he had smacked the side with the flat of his hand. Faded turquoise paint flaked around the windows and cactus-spike gouges were etched low on the sides.

"Looks like it's been rode hard and put up wet," Reggie had commented.

Liv had brought banana nut bread to me several times in the last few months. She knew the pot plants were just at the edge of the woods. She knew I smoked the marijuana medicinally, to help relieve the pain in my chest from the coughing and the arthritic ache in my hands, knees, neck and shoulders; pain caused from years of lifting heavy parts, standing at odd angles over a car's fender, reaching up into the engine.

Liv also knew I sold a little on the side. My hours at Ross' service station had been cut back, and the income from the plants helped me pay my rent. Colorado was one of eleven states that had decriminalized small amounts of marijuana in 1973. I thought that by helping Reggie grow half a dozen plants, I was well under the radar, well within the acceptable limits.

Late one especially hot, dry August afternoon, I returned from the AA meeting in the large cool basement room of the Methodist church. I was carrying a Styrofoam cup half-full of black coffee as I walked to the edge of the woods. I almost screeched to a stop when I saw that all the plants had been pulled up, thrown on the ground and stomped on. Sweat broke out under my baseball cap and my heart raced, my chest vibrated. The now-lukewarm coffee made a perfect split-second arc as I flung it into the air. It landed with a splat on the dry ground. With almost one motion, I crumpled the cup and stuffed it into the front pocket of my blue and brown plaid shirt.

I gathered up the debilitated plants and stacked them, one on top of the other. I stuffed them tightly against the base of a large fir tree where I hoped the drooping branches would hide them. I took off the battered Rockies cap and picked some tightly folded bills from the inside band. I walked the two miles to Karl Debrosse's greenhouse where I bought six more plants.

Three days later, when the scenario repeated itself, I got the message; the law knew where the plants were growing. I gathered up the nearly lifeless plants and stuffed them into a thick black plastic trash bag. I walked two-thirds of a mile to the 7-11 on the highway and tossed the bag into the giant, dark green dumpster.

I went back to the trailer, stuffed the remaining cash into the worn baseball cap's inside band, packed clothes, a toothbrush and a few camping necessities into my backpack. Under a chipped but clean-scrubbed coffee mug on the kitchen table, I left the key, a note and some cash for the landlady. I went to Liv's.

She and Brian had a key to their landlord's storage shed in the back yard of their little rented house. Even though Brian didn't like it, Liv let me sleep there.

"Well, what am I supposed to do, Brian? I can't make him sleep in a ditch somewhere when he could be safe and dry here. The shed's not fancy but it keeps him out of the elements. It doesn't seem like too much for him to ask of me. He was really good to Mom and to me when I was young and he was really nice about the whole wedding thing – it's almost like I owe him this one little favor. And it won't be for long." Lavinia had appealed to her husband as I sat waiting on the front stoop.

Brian adjusted his glasses, lowered his chin and hugged his shoulders upwards as if trying to insulate his feelings. They had just discovered that Liv was pregnant and Brian knew an argument – any argument - could turn into tears. I guess he decided it was not worth it. That evening, while Brian was in the classroom, Liv gave me the key. I put my sleeping bag and backpack inside and to the right, just behind the shed's door.

During the day, I walked in the woods or helped a friend work on a car. In the evenings, which seemed to begin earlier and earlier, I hung around the bars with Reggie. Often I staggered back to the shed and crashed. The arrangement kept me safe for almost three weeks.

One afternoon about three, Liv and I were sitting under a cloudless sky in mis-matched folding chairs on the concrete slab patio out behind the Spartan little house. We heard Noreen's SUV pull into the gravel driveway. I coughed and rubbed my arthritic knee as I got up. I dashed to the shed, went in and gently pushed the door almost shut. Noreen's car door slammed.

I saw Liv glance down to see a cigarette butt with a tiny glowing ember, left in the ashtray on the patio table. She grunted her weight out of the lawn chair, webbing imprints on the back of her legs, and walked toward her mother. The two women hugged and Noreen rubbed the expanding abdomen.

"You're getting big."

"Yeah, they tell me that happens."

"You feeling ok?"

"Well, carrying the extra weight doesn't help my ankle. It hurts most of the time."

"Damn Ken for getting you into that awful accident. I'll never forgive him and I doubt you can either. Travis and I've talked to a lawyer about it and he agrees with us. Ken is responsible. If you decided to sue, you could win a lawsuit."

"Oh, Mom, you know he doesn't have any money. Cm'on, let's sit inside." The two women walked, arms around each other, into the little house.

Half of my right eye watched through a crack in the

door. I saw Noreen turn and glance over her shoulder first at the table and chairs and do then a quick scan of the shed. I couldn't tell if she knew I was in there or not but I knew then that I had to leave. Noreen would be furious with Liv if I got caught there.

Chapter Eighteen

"Ken," Liv's green eyes flashed at me as she spoke, "what do you want to do about all this?" She sat down and leaned back on the used navy-blue Naugahyde sofa and it gave a little *whoosh* under her weight. She shifted, trying to find a comfortable place for the almost-baby.

"Everyone around here knows that pot is sort of legal - but sort of not." Her hands spread smooth circles around her belly. "Well, everyone but Travis. I guess he's kind of hard-nosed about it. Could you just tell him that you took over Uncle Reggie's plants and you were growing for your own use, that it helps the pain in your shoulders and neck?" She pressed one hand against the tiny movement that showed on the surface of her large cotton shirt. "Umph," she said and took a breath, "I mean, you have to do something."

"Livie, honey, you know I can't talk to Travis. He'd throw me in jail - *under* the jail if he had his way. He's in charge and he makes sure growers are not treated kindly in his jurisdiction. You'd think it wouldn't be a serious crime anymore. I mean, this is 1999, not 1969." I didn't say it but I really wanted to see the baby born, to hold my grandchild - Liv's child - in my arms. "You know I've got six more plants but nobody else knows. That kind of thing always comes out in a small town. Once word gets out and with your mama married Travis, I don't have much chance."

My head fell into my hands and I ran my fingers through my hair, still thick and dark and only sparsely spotted with grey in my middle age. I got up and paced the floor of the tidy little house. I gripped the edge of the small wear-yellowed kitchen sink. My arms were rigid and braced me as my head hung down, my chin nearly touching the first buttonhole of the much-worn plaid flannel shirt.

"Ken," Liv sighed and spoke to me firmly, "I respect your choices. But I expect you know what will happen. If you run and Travis chases you down, he'll have no trouble arresting you. He wants to be the Colorado sheriff with the most drug arrests and I'm pretty sure that if you keep growing in this county, you're going to be one of them. I don't think Mom's exactly filled his head with happy stories about you." She shifted her weight again. "Mmmm," she said and her mouth tightened for a few seconds as the baby moved.

"I know you want to help us but Brian's getting his master's. He's sure to get tenure and we'll be ok. We will." She said this in a flat tone, like she was reciting a story I already knew. "But I can't help you anymore. You've been here three weeks and you need to find someplace else. And you can't just disappear."

I felt her gaze, warm on my back, so deep and steady that it belied her 21 years. I love you like you're my own because in my heart, you are, I thought, just as I had for possibly a billion times during her life. I knew I couldn't risk having Noreen angry at Liv – the girl did not need that right now. My head lifted and I dropped my hands to my side. I turned in her direction and we looked directly at each other.

"Where are your car keys, honey? It's better if you don't know where I am or even which way I'm headed. Just drop me off at Humphries, I'll leave from there."

Inside Winter Park's biggest store, I reached for the metal handle of a maroon collapsible canvas basket, dark maroon in color. I put it back as I realized I'd need a shopping cart to go through the aisles. Just because my eyes rested on them, I tossed a large bottle of Tylenol into the cart. In the camping area, I picked up an aluminum cooking pot and a Butane stove with two fuel cans.

I was headed into the mountains, didn't know how long I'll be there. Guess I might need to cook. What else? I added a roll of duct tape, a yellow-green plastic poncho, and a green camping pillow to the cart.

As I stood in the checkout line behind a young mom pushing a cart filled with a tow-headed toddler and two bright red boxes of pull-ups, I tugged my wallet out of my back pocket. From the vertical display on the right, I chose a packaged comb.

Right next to the combs was *People* magazine. There, on the bright, glossy cover, I saw Rick Wilkes, star of the new Hollywood action blockbuster. I picked up the magazine and held it with both hands.

I guess nobody calls him Little Dickie anymore and that makes me smile. He always said he'd get out of MacKremmon and he did.

His dad never accepted Dickie after he came out – he died without every speaking to his oldest son again. But Dickie had flown his mother to Hollywood several times and even escorted her down the red carpet. She had bragged on her 'little Dickie' and his film career until her death just three years ago. As far as anyone knew, Rick had never returned to MacKremmon, not even for a visit.

Good for him. It couldn't have been easy. I

remembered the way Dickie had been teased and harassed by other boys, starting in fifth grade and going all the way through high school. The muscular boys in cowboy shirts and jeans made fun of Dickie's brightly colored clothing, of the "product" he wore in his hair, the batik coin purse he carried in his jeans pocket. From the back pages of a movie magazine, Dickie had ordered a keychain featuring a tiny Oscar charm on it. The bulked up boys made a habit of flushing it down the toilet at school. He must have bought a dozen of them because every week, Dickie had another one.

He was part of the MacKremmon saga but he changed his story. He won. He did it his way. I'm glad for him. I replaced the glossy publication and coughed.

When the phlegmy crash from my lungs subsided, I took several deep breaths and brought my mind back to the present. A perky young cashier with a tiny silver ring through her nostril, was already ringing up my purchases. I handed over cash to pay the bill and hefted a large plastic bag in each hand as I left Humphries. I chewed the inside of my cheek as I forgot about Dickie – I craved a cigarette. Cigarettes – I knew I would need them. I went to the Mountain Food Store where I bought five cartons, the state's limit.

I walked two miles due east of the store. I juggled the bags and smoked one cigarette after another, each one lighting the next in line. My stomach growled and I realized I hadn't thought much about food until that moment. A flimsy white plastic bag with red lettering that said "Thank you for shopping at Humphries" was squishy full and gripped in one hand. Another bag bounced when my right elbow bent as my hand ferried the cigarette to and from my lips via a bent-arm arc. A larger bag, equally full but with sharp angles protruding and stretching the white plastic, was slung over each of my shoulders.

I carried the bags to the sun-faded red pick-up,

Reggie's pick-up, that I had hidden deep in the stand of lodgepole pines just a couple of weeks earlier. The truck bed was grimy and, when I tossed the bags into it, coughed up powdery dust. I pulled up a green dome tent and covered the lumpy pile.

Out of the truck bed, I picked up a Colorado Rockies baseball cap, black fading to runny streaks of gunmetal grey; it had been Reggie's. I stuffed some carefully folded bills into the inside band and put the cap on. Frayed strings spilt down around the edges of the stiff bill. The top of the *R* had come unstitched so it drooped down, away from the cap, clinging by a thread. I tugged the cap low over my eyes. I snapped the $9.99 price tag off the new sunglasses before I put them on. I was careful to keep the tags and smoked down cigarette butts in a zip-up plastic bag. I didn't want anyone following an easy trail to me.

I drove the plodding old Chevy truck about two miles along Virginia Canyon Road to a spot where a rundown convenience store balanced lonely on the right. I bought another five cartons of Camels and dropped the plastic bag onto the truck seat next to me.

Can't take a chance on running out, don't know how long I'll be out here. Might even need to ration my smokes. That realization quickened my heartbeat and gave me the shakes. Noreen had always called me obsessive compulsive, but that didn't begin to describe my smoking habit. Even if I was not lighting a cigarette, I had to have a package of smokes in view, near to hand at all times. It was just one of the million things that hadn't bothered Noreen when we met but seemed to drive her crazier and crazier every year we were married.

I didn't want to risk being seen by Sheriff Nolen's deputies who might be patrolling the isolated area so I chose an out-of-the-way diner, an old converted service station, whose windows were hooded in once-warm grease. It was the last stop before the woods and was frequented mostly during the season by camouflage-clad hunters whose trucks showed a rack, evidence of a successful trip. I nosed the pick-up into a space in the back, near the 50-gallon oil drum the owner used for burning trash. I turned off the ignition and the road-weary engine quit with a quaking so severe I felt my internal organs vibrate. I coughed.

Inside the cafe, I propped my elbows on the clammy beige countertop. I snubbed out my cigarette in the thin metal ashtray and ordered.

I thought this could be my last restaurant meal for awhile. I'd soon be eating only my own cooking.

Steam rose from the bowl of chili with hatch peppers. It was an easy fit, a comfortable-old-chair kind of choice. Butter pooled onto the biscuit and I ate, thinking about my childhood where chili was the staple. I smiled to myself as I remembered wondering, as a boy, if Daddy had known how to cook anything else.

Chapter Nineteen

THE DINER'S SIGNATURE DESSERT was choke cherry pie with a flaky, homemade crust. I ate two slices and ordered chili to go. The stubble-faced counterman poured the chili into a deep Styrofoam cup, spilling a little next to a yellow stain on the once-white apron, and snapped a plastic lid into place around the rim. He packed the cup and two foil-wrapped biscuits into a brown paper grocery bag and folded down the top neatly. I paid the tab.

"That oughta hold you till an early dinner." The counterman showed a gap-toothed smile as he handed me the change.

"You'd think. Thanks." I left the coins on the counter and carried the bag outside.

I set the future meal down by the left rear tire. From the truck bed, I picked up a screwdriver, which I used to take the green and white Colorado license plates off first the back and then the front of the old truck. Out of my backpack, I tugged a worn remnant of dark green wool blanket. I wrapped the metal plates in it. I stuck the flat bundle into the trash barrel and buried it under a layer of flaky grey ash, cardboard cartons and crumpled paper napkins, heavy with mustard and grease stains. I shook the cigarette butts and receipts out of the zip-up bag and using a twig from the overhanging cottonwood, carefully stirred them in among the charred remains.

I got in the truck and the door shut with a weak clink. I put the takeout bag on the passenger seat next to me and drove three-quarters of a mile down the forsaken gravel road. I pulled the truck off to the left, onto a rocky patch overhung with branches of a tall fir tree, a spot often used as a parking area by local hunters. The truck could be there for a week or more before it was noticed. Until then, no one would think anything of it.

I knew the ten essentials and spent nearly forty-five minutes repacking my backpack, making sure first-aid supplies, fire starter matches, a map of the area, a compass, a knife, and extra clothing fit snugly inside. I adjusted the pack straps over my shoulders, hefted the plastic bags of cigarettes, grabbed up the brown paper bag containing the dinner, and threw a quick appreciative glance back at the now unidentifiable truck. Then I turned west and made my way back down the steep rocky road to Highway 81.

I had snagged half a cardboard box from the diner's trash heap and hand-lettered a sign that read "Arapahoe by Nightfall." I walked a little over a mile back, in the direction I'd come, and held up the sign. I stuck out my thumb. I'd smoked several cigarettes and was reaching into the backpack for a fleece as the end-of-the-sunshine chill threatened to turn raw through my thin flannel shirt.

That's when a beat-up old Subaru station wagon pulled over. From the driver's seat, the voice seemed to be sandwiched between a worn dark brown fedora and a scraggly grey beard when it said, "You don't mind Ranger, do ya?" I glanced at the German Shepherd who lay in the wayback, eyes wide, head down between his paws. I shook my head.

"Then hop in," said the man. "I'm going as far as the Kawuneeche Visitors' Center. I bet you can get a ride from there. Where you headed?"

"There are a couple of good campsites in Arapahoe," I replied.

"Arapahoe National Forest? What's that, about a thousand square miles? Gets cold up there, doesn't it?" asked the driver.

"Yeah, the views are really something and I'm hoping to see some pronghorns," I nodded and lit a cigarette and coughed.

"The cold won't help that cough," the driver commented. The car was old and I could feel the weak springs in the seat just under me.

By the time we reached Kawuneeche Visitors' Center, dark had settled like thick eyelids that closed out the day's light. Tourists' RVs and sport utility vehicles had all pulled out of the parking lot, leaving the yellow lines forming toothless gaps.

"Thanks," I said as I closed the passenger door of the car. The heel of his hand stayed on the wheel as the driver lifted his fingers in a half wave. The dog stood up in the back and turned to look at me as the car pulled away.

The door was locked and the interior of the windowed, flat visitors' center building was dark. There was an adobe wall about three feet high going around the right side of the building. That would have been a good place to stow away for the night but an orange plastic cone marked a pile of dirt. Obviously, some kind of digging was underway, maybe plumbing repair work. Good thing I knew my way around here.

I picked up my gear and walked back down the road. I crossed the road, empty of traffic in the early darkling, and turned right. I hiked up a gentle rocky incline to the cemetery where the gravesites were uneven and shaggy. Nature seemed to be slowly reclaiming them, the marked ones and the unmarked ones, by dropping brown pine needles and spiky cones in a thick, uneven and relentless pattern. Where it had once probably been sharply delineated, the cemetery now stretched and sprawled over the land; only murky boundaries existed.

My shoulders shrugged to redistribute the weight of the backpack and ease the almost constant ache. Around me I saw manicured granite headstones, one with an angel and two with Celtic crosses carved deep into them. Words and names were carefully etched for all eternity. Further on, my eyes paused on an uneven circle of rocks that looked like they had been arranged by an unsure child or an adult with a shaky hand. At what might have been the top of the circle was a small wooden sign, attached to a wooden tongue depressor, with one word written in black uneven letters, '*Unknown.*'

Just beyond and to the left of the mangy edges of the lopsided graveyard, a cottonwood about twenty feet tall had fallen over, probably the result of a heavy summer thunderstorm. The shaggy top end of the tree rested on a large pink granite boulder. I tucked the shopping bags and my backpack under the horizontal roof it created.

Even cold, the diner chili was good. My fingers were stiff with arthritis and the round red lid on the bottle wasn't easy for me to open but I did it. I tossed two white tablets into my mouth and took a big gulp from my water bottle to wash them down. I could hear the wind lisping in the aspen leaves as I untied the sleeping bag and crawled into the unrolled comfort. I snuggled down into it.

I rubbed my neck, squeezed my shoulder blades together and up toward my ears, and released them. The ibuprofen did its job and I fell asleep. In my dream, the Subaru driver told Travis where he'd dropped me off and the

Sheriff had come looking for me. As the patrol car came to a screeching stop in front of my sleeping spot, I woke up from the dream, yelling. I breathed heavily as I got up, scratched my head with both hands, staggered a few steps into the woods. I looked at the stars and felt my mind clear. I walked back to the sleeping bag and crawled in.

In the morning, I headed to the visitors' center and cleaned up in the men's room. Park rangers don't encourage hitchhikers so I milled around the parking. Getting a ride up into the forest was no problem. I took the ragged Rockies cap out of the backpack and set it low over my eyes. I backed myself onto the low stonewall, where I sat casually looking out onto cars as they pulled in.

In ninth grade, we had learned that in the early 1900's, Arapahoe National Forest had been declared the nation's first forest preserve. Every year since then, it had been one of the most visited recreation sites in the county. Close access to Fraser, Silverthorne and Granby made it easy for hikers, campers and nature lovers to enjoy its beauty. Birders were especially interested and they might see Sora, Virginia rails, Wilson's phalarope, American avocet and other species. I've heard that even great blue heron nested there.

I had smoked three cigarettes when a dark green Toyota Corolla with two bikes mounted on top pulled into the lot. I noticed that the two young men in the car took turns going into the center. That way, one of them was always with the bikes, which I figured were expensive.

"Nice bikes," I said and ground out my cigarette.

"Yeah," said the guy in the passenger seat, "only in Colorado are the bikes worth twice what the car carrying them is." Both men laughed easily. "There's space in the backseat if you need a ride. We're going up the road."

"You cycle?" asked the driver, as he glanced back at me sitting in the backseat next to neat piles of helmets, gloves, lightweight parkas and water bottles.

"Naw," I replied, "my old bones can't take bike riding anymore. Wait till you pass 40 and your knees give out, your hands have trouble gripping the handlebars and your shoulders hurt, you'll see what I mean." I coughed and both guys laughed appreciatively. They teased me about being "over the hill" during the drive.

"Just up ahead, yeah, there, pull over right there, if you would."

The driver bumped the car gently off the edge of the road.

"Thanks for the ride," I said as I slammed the door. The driver stuck his arm out the car window and waved as the top-heavy Toyota pulled back onto the road. I hefted the backpack and bags and hiked east to a spot I knew, one where I'd taken Liv years ago when we camped together.

Chapter Twenty

Cool nights were hard on the tightness in my chest. But the chilly air did help give me a sense of energy. I moved my campsite a couple of times but stayed within sight of the spot that held memories for me. I noticed the eerie legacy, a skeletal forest of dead spruce and once true-green fir that stretched across the higher slopes below the tundra and remembered my father's talk of the 1940's bark beetle epidemic.

I knew that forests with high densities of large trees were susceptible to mountain pine beetles. For a couple of years, winter temperatures had not been cold enough to kill the larva and as the spring brought more and more mature bugs, the outbreak peaked and the trees became dry and milkfish-blue color of older eyes. Larger trees were killed, too. Thousands of trees had been lost and the forest's appearance was still one of a ghostly, almost other-worldly landscape. The scorched overhead branches often made me think of photos I'd seen as a boy, photos of a cathedral that been burned out, the roof missing and charred roof pieces black against the sky while the heart of the church, the pews, icons, the altar, the spiritual aura, remained.

I'd been in the woods for seven days, each one meandered like a road that starts out going somewhere but ends up being open scenery. Every day I walked for an hour or so, and it seemed to take more and more effort of my laboring lungs. My breaths staggered, shortened. Often, I walked in a trance-like state so while my hiking boots carried my daily-diminishing weight over piles of fall leaves, across tiny streams and around pre-historic boulders, tender almost sacrosanct pictures of childhood played movie-like in my mind.

Walks I had taken as a child through the woods had inspired an awe of nature and I saw my younger self holding my breath and hiding behind a big rock to watch a large-antlered elk lift his head toward the sun and bugle his dominance. I saw silver fish flash in rushing stream waters. I saw vibrant sunsets over glistening water. My mother was right – I had been baptized by nature. That sacred rite had sensitized me to every aspect of the natural world, made me want to be a communicant, be enveloped, cloaked, comforted by nature's rites and her daily spiritual expressions. I was steeped in the scent of the woods.

As I sat, water bottle in hand, the conversation I'd had with Reggie came to mind. We were at Kate's for an early lunch.

"I'm buying," Reggie had told me. "We're celebrating."

"Celebrating what?" At that moment, the waitress appeared, order pad in hand.

""I'll have a bacon cheeseburger all the way." Reggie tilted his head and gave her his most charming grin. "And what time do you get off tonight?" He winked.

She sighed. She'd heard it all before.

"Reggie, cut it out. You want that medium-rare like always?"

Reggie nodded and I ordered. The waitress brought two beers and set them down without looking at either of us. We talked about the upcoming ski season until the food arrived.

Reggie ordered another beer. He drained the last few drops of golden liquid from the thick, cold glass and handed it to the waitress. She set a fresh, foaming mug down on the table. She didn't look at him this time, either.

"Well, I've had a lot of fun in Colorado winters, you know I have, but I've decided I'm kinda tired of the cold," Reggie told me. "I think I'm ready for a change - and I've met somebody. Her name is Esperanza and she's from Mexico but she lives in south Florida, down near Miami. If everything works out right, I'm going to marry her and move to the Sunshine State."

"You what?" The knife slid out of my surprised fingers and hit the thick china plate with a *thunk*. I put both forearms on the table and leaned over, closer to Reggie. "Seriously? You're gonna get married? And you think you might leave here?"

"Yeah, bro, I do. I keep thinking of something you said years ago about not letting Mama's leaving us turn us into hardened men who don't trust women. I want to trust Esperanza. I *do* trust her. And I think I love her." Reggie drank half the beer in one gulp and swiped the back of his weather-splotched hand across his mouth.

"Yeah, I'm pretty sure I do. I've known a lot of women, you know I have. Hell, I've poked anything female on two legs." Embarrassed pride came into his half-grin. He took another gulp of Coors. I nodded but I couldn't think what to say.

"I met Essie at that ski equipment expo in Reno three months ago and she's a looker. I think I'm ready to settle down. Yeah, I think she's the one."

He held the burger in his hand and took a bite of it. He chewed and put the sandwich down.

I shook my head and coughed. "Jeeze, I … uh … I guess nobody knows what someone else is thinking – even brothers. I'm going to need a minute to take all of this in. Seems kind of sudden like."

"Yeah, I hear you." Reggie swallowed. "Well, Essie needs to marry a US citizen. I've got my share of the money from the sale of the house. You know I've lived rent-free for years and I spent some of it on, uh, stuff but I've still got nearly all of it." He wiped his mouth and shot me a look. "And I've got a lead on a job working in a water ski equipment shop – those people in Florida water ski a lot. We can buy a house and well, you know, live a good life together." Reggie finished the beer. He put the empty mug down and dipped a fried onion ring into a messy mound of ketchup. "Might even have a couple of kids," he grinned.

He signaled for another beer. "And you'll take care of my plants, right? There are only a few and you know where they are."

"Well, growing has never been my goal but yeah, I'll take care of your plants. Anyway, a puff or two always helps my joints – it's too bad I had to quit growing my own." I looked back down at the steak and eggs. I shook a little salt onto the steady glare of the fried yellow yolk-eye. "Yeah, I'll tend your plants. So what's Esperanza like? I'd sure like to meet the woman who got you to settle down."

I had checked daily on the six marijuana plants Reggie had nursed. But I did not get to meet Esperanza before Reggie left. He had vacated his little apartment, left his skis and snowshoes on consignment, and donated his winter clothes to Goodwill. He had signed the title of his old pick-up over to me. I had given Reggie a loud Hawaiian shirt from Humphries. I had hugged my brother good-bye and watched him get on the bus that would take him to the Denver airport and a plane to Miami.

Two weeks later, a postcard featuring long-necked, hoof-forward racing horses on an oval track with bright pink flamingoes in the middle told me that Reggie and Esperanza were married in a quiet service at Iglesia Catolica Santa Barbara in Hialeah.

Now I need to get deeper into the woods. I need to breathe in the scent of the woods, the oily essence of the pines, the dry fragrance of the aspen, the scratchy aroma of cottonwood, the sweetness of the redbud.

In my mind, pictures of Reggie and me as little kids elbowed each other for space – Reggie playing with Tooley, Reggie swinging the plump red sock, Reggie with a towel tied around his neck jumping off the roof of the shed, Reggie, Reggie. Now he was a married man who'd probably have a family of his own one day. I wasn't the all-important brother anymore. That was the natural order of things but still I felt low.

Most afternoons a tiredness oozes from deep inside me. It loosens my limbs and erases my energy. I often take ibuprofen to lessen the hurt in my chest and grinding almost metallic aches in my knees. Then I settle into the sleeping bag for a nap. Later in the day, I read, breathe in the woodsy smells and sketch in the notebook my parents gave me long ago. Food is losing its appeal and I think my taste buds are draining away like old motor oil. As dark eases in, I open cans of food and eat the contents cold, avoiding for just a little longer the need to build a campfire. Through it all, I smoke steadily and I think about life, the story of my life, the story everyone in MacKremmon knew or thought they did.

Nuts and trail mix are my daily breakfast ration. I fill my water bottle from a sputtering waterfall about a hundred yards upstream where the clear water smashes itself over smooth rocks. Soon the mornings will be chilly enough for a fire and coffee.

I sit smoking, coughing, thinking and watching the pile of cigarettes diminish and that makes me nervous.

Chapter Twenty-One

Two days ago, I looked at the sun and judged it was about two in the afternoon. In the dry leaves that signaled full-on fall, I heard a crackling, like cellophane being wadded up in a fist. I was sitting on the sleeping bag and my head snapped around. My eyes widened in sudden surprise when I saw Noreen. Sudden adrenalin pushed me up onto my feet. She was walking toward me, head down, hair swinging. She was heavier now but for a split second, she looked to my mind just like she did years ago when she threw her shapely legs over the braces of the wooden picnic table. Her head leaned forward and her hair swung in step. In her right hand was a large plastic bag.

"Hey, Ken." As she looked up, I noticed her hair had been cut shorter and even though it was mostly grey now, it was still thick and beautiful.

"Dr. Livingstone, I presume." She smiled. "You used to tell me your mother said that to you." The plastic bag in her hand moved rhymically with a casual sexy-swishy sound. "Thought you might be needing these by now." The tone of Noreen's voice was relaxed and fluid, as if she had seen me at the dinner table only yesterday.

I gave a half nod. My suspicious side stood straight up but my eyes and my mind clamped onto the bag she was carrying. It contained cartons of cigarettes. Noreen glanced around and found a grassy spot under an aspen tree just across from my sleeping bag. She sat down and dumped two brown and white rectangular packages out of the bag. She picked up a carton gently like it was some delicate material instead of cardboard.

"Good god, Noreen, I'm nearly shocked to death to see you."

My heartbeat jolted and caused my chest to rise and fall rapidly. I was thin and the skin rumbled over protruding ribs. I was quivering all over. I hoped she didn't notice I held my arms folded across my chest to steady the trembling. My hands spread themselves over my bony rib cage and my face froze. Suddenly, I tore my eyes from the bag and blinked. It occurred to me that she might not have come alone and I jerked my head from side to side, searching. She might have brought someone with her, the sheriff maybe.

"What are you doing here? You by yourself?"

"Of course I am. Who'd want to come way out here with me?"

I trusted my senses that we were alone and the internal pounding slowed.

"Yeah, well, thanks for the smokes." I eased down onto the old brown sleeping bag. I rubbed my knees and looked at her.

"No problem, Ken," she replied easily. She gave me a little smile. "How're you doing? I bet the nights are already cool up here in these elevations," she said and nodded toward my knees. She glanced down briefly and indicated the ragged sleeping bag where I sat. "Looks like you've been writing in your wildflower log. You've had that a long time, haven't you?"

The dark brown leather book lay on the sleeping bag. The once-blank pages were now full of details I had recorded, sketches I'd made, thoughts I wanted to keep that might help me figure things out; parts of my story I wanted to mull over and maybe one day share. The pages looked puffed up now, like they were showing off their fullness, promoting their own consequence, fulfilling their mission of illustrating a life.

"I wanted you to have the cigarettes." She tossed the carton toward me. "I know you can't be without them. It can't be good for your lungs to smoke like you do but I guess after thirty-something years, you're not about to quit, are you? *C'est la vie*," she said in her best French. "How've you been?"

"Ok, good, yeah, I'm good." I reached over and picked up the carton by the corner. I gazed at it like it was a sacred object. Then my view slid to Noreen.

"Well, I guess you've got enough cigarettes for awhile." Noreen's head tilted toward her shoulder, almost a posture of pity.

"Uhh, thanks." From the zippered front compartment of my backpack, I pulled a small rectangular box of matches. I flipped up the top of the cigarette pack and remembered the day when wrapping the clear cellophane made a sound like the crackle of a tiny fire. Over my index finger, I tapped out a single cigarette and put it to my lips. The match scratched the flame into existence. I lit the cigarette and blew smoke out. As I took a second puff, I suddenly bent forward – a series of coughs hacked their way up from my lungs, and jumped ragged into the air. Finally, I took my hand away from my mouth.

"Are you ok?"

"I'm fine." I shook my head and sat up as straight as I could. "I'm fine."

"Is it pneumonia? Lung cancer, do you think?"

"Hell, what difference does it make, Noreen? I've

smoked all my life. For years, I was too busy to go to a doctor. Then I didn't have insurance. So I don't know but I'd guess my lungs are shot."

"Ken, I don't have any hard feelings toward you. You know that, right?" Noreen leaned forward.

"Yeah, I guess. But what are you doing here?" I flicked ash onto a bare spot of ground.

"Oh, I just told Travis I was going to drive over and see Maroon Bells. He didn't bat an eye. So here I am."

"How did you find me?" I coughed twice.

"Finding you wasn't that hard," she said. "Lavinia remembered your favorite camping places. I think she wanted to come with me to see you. But I finally got her to tell me the locations. I guess I just knew how to ask. I've spent some time, driving to each site and checking it out until I found this spot – and you."

"So what did you have to give her so she'd tell you about the campsites and not come with you?"

"Well, she and Brian are outgrowing that rented bungalow and they need a real house. Let's just say they'll get plenty of room for a growing family in return for some information I wanted."

I nodded. Noreen had known what it took to get Liv to do what she wanted. Giving Liv things to keep control of the situation was nothing new for Noreen.

"Is Livie's baby here yet?"

"Actually, she wanted me to tell you. She and Brian had a little boy last Sunday. They've named him Dawson."

I perked up. My whole body seemed to straighten a bit.

"Really? Dawson?"

"Yes, she wanted you to know. She said you were always good to her and no matter how things turned out, she wanted to honor that." Noreen's shoulder shrugged slightly. "Besides, it was the only name she and Brian could agree on."

My weakening heart seemed stronger, seemed to grow a little inside me. A baby boy – named after me, my family – a boy with my mother's name. I felt my chest expand with the validation of it all.

"Here," Noreen pulled two photos out of her back pocket. "Lavinia sent these to you." The little cheekbones were rosy and bright on the newborn's face.

"He looks a little like you, Noreen."

Noreen nodded and I noticed the wrinkled skin on her neck. I held the photos, tilted my head back and exhaled cigarette smoke into the sky. Then I looked again at the little face and smiled.

"Well," she closed her arms across her chest, like she was holding something in, "you were always good to Lavinia – and to me – and I guess I just feel, I don't know, like I need to tell you that and not leave it unsaid. In some ways, I feel a little bad about how things turned out." She unlatched her arms and reached up under her thick hair to scratch the back of her neck. Then she put her hands primly in her lap. I noticed her perfectly manicured nails.

"Well, I loved Liv like she was my own. And I loved you, Noreen, I did – that's why I married you." I looked down at the burned ash, a tiny red light in the tobacco. My chin jutted forward as I looked at her.

"Kenny, you are sweet and trusting, aren't you?" A forced patience was in her voice, as if she were talking to a child. "Did you really think I didn't know about the pot plants? I knew you had some and I knew for years that Reggie had them."

"What?" I felt my eyebrows bump together. "Hell, I guess I was just so caught up in living life and running the shops that I … I just … didn't give it much thought." I lifted the old baseball cap, scratched my head and settled the cap back in place. "I guess you could have told Travis at any time."

It all seemed muddled. Events that happened years ago raced through my mind. The facts couldn't seem to keep pace. I reached over and ground out the cigarette stub in the prehistoric soil.

"I knew Reggie was growing and selling. I confronted him and he paid me not to tell, not to tell on you or on him. And I wanted more – for Lavinia – and for me – so the money came in handy." She held her head straight up on her neck. Her back was rigid like she was posing for a picture, an indelible one for my mind to save.

"You blackmailed my brother? You took money to keep quiet about the pot plants?"

"It wasn't a lot of money so it didn't bother me at first," she paused. "But now, well, I'm not proud of it. I just felt like I wanted to tell you now so we can get it out in the open. Besides, he had all that money from the sale of the house. It's not like he was broke."

I was getting the picture and I couldn't stand to look at her.

"You knew Travis could get Reggie for growing. It'd look like we were users and maybe I was a dealer. People would think I was just a drunk, a pothead and no damn good. They'd think how lucky for you and Liv that you'd married Travis." I lit another cigarette and exhaled the smoke. I watched as it spiraled itself upward toward the top of a red needled pine.

"I'd probably have gone to jail and been out of your life. But that would have been an embarrassment for you. Is that about right? That why you married Travis?"

"Well, his green eyes had something to do with it but I guess that's close enough," she replied blushing a little.

"And you're right, I couldn't have you in jail. Think what that would mean for Lavinia's social life." She paused and examined the large diamond ring on her left hand. "I mean, Travis is a Nolen. You know they are practically the founding family of MacKremmon." Her nose lifted and she sniffed. I thought of an oil painting of someone's ancestor, the kind tourists like to find at flea markets.

"Ken, I know your mother left and you always felt like she abandoned you. And I expect you felt that way when Lavinia and I moved out." She put both arms straight behind her and propped herself straight up. "But in many ways, it's like it had nothing to do with you. Did you ever think maybe it was just your fate?"

"Huh? I don't get it."

"Your mother didn't leave because of anything you did or didn't do. Neither did Lavinia and I. It always seemed like you were trying really hard to get us to love you." She stopped and picked imaginary fuzz off her left knee.

"There were just certain things that happened and it seemed to you like they were destined to happen to you. Those things just happened, and you didn't necessarily do anything to deserve them. You knew I was pregnant when we got married and you really did do your best to provide for Lavinia and me. You tried real hard – you did and I saw that. I expect you tried real hard with your mother, too. And when those relationships didn't work out, well, instead of saying *c'est la vie*, you took it all to heart. But things don't always work out and that's how life is sometimes. Does that make any sense?" Noreen looked at me and there was a softening at the corners of her mouth.

"What? Good god, no, it doesn't make any sense. What are you talking about, Noreen? This is my life and not some damn bumper sticker." My teeth gritted themselves together, my jaw tightened. "That's it? That's all you've got for an explanation – this kind of crap happens? I was doomed?" I inhaled the cigarette, took two big puffs, one right after another. My thin, ridged chest heaved and trembled.

Had I always had a deep, far-away sense that my mother's abandonment wasn't wholly and totally my fault?

Had my father's passive acceptance molded my own responses? Had the dynamics of life that had carried me along the turbulence brought me to this point? Had I taken all the hurt and desertion to heart and never spent time figuring out how to deal with it? Was I now, in my late forties beginning to think my parents were only human, that they made mistakes? If I could forgive my friends, could I forgive my parents? Had they lived in another time, might they have done things differently?

"Do you think you'll ever forgive your mother for leaving? I mean, it's up to you. It happened a long time ago and with Reggie gone, you're the one who has to deal with it."

Could I forgive my mother for leaving? When she left, it was like strong intertwined hands suddenly weakened, lessened, loosened and I fell out of the grip, fell with dizzying speed and then in slow motion. Her abandonment of our family had shaped my entire life. I'd married Noreen partly to prove that I could get past being left, to have a family, to be part of a closeness, to wipe out that sense of being lonely and alone. But Noreen and Liv had left, too. Now Liv had a child, someone who would grow into an adult with the secure love of a family and the confidence that comes with that. In some convoluted way, I wondered, did that somehow make sense, offer some hope for the future?

Noreen paused and took a slow panoramic look around the deep woods. "You've always loved being in the woods, haven't you? You trust nature," she said, changing the subject.

Neither of us spoke for a moment and then she said, "You don't look so good. But I guess you're perfectly fine out here. It's like the woods are strong enough to hold you and comfort you. You planning to stay for awhile?"

"Naw, I'm not staying. But I'm ok for right now." I felt tired, like a weightiness in my bones, felt it as an unpleasant immensity in my muscles, my skin, my whole body. I wanted to feel safe in the forest, wanted to feel it secured me, held me true and constant in its heart, without any more effort on my part; I just didn't have any energy left.

If she told Travis where I was, he might decide to come for me, split the forest open. The woods would betray me, divulge my camp and glaringly show me out, give me up.

I had to start thinking, planning what to do next. I aimed to walk farther west where the aspen clumped and trees grew thick as blades of grass on a lawn, where the undergrowth had been mushed into compost for thousands of years, where casual hikers rarely went, where they were discouraged by the shawl of the forest falling over them and where the blackness of the nights could shut out thoughts of new dawn. After I saw more of the forest, after I'd pulled mountain air into my wasting lungs, after I'd been revitalized by the scent of the wild, I'd go back to MacKremmon. I'd go see Liv's baby.

I had almost forgotten Noreen was sitting there. At this time of year, we were the only people for miles around. For several minutes, there was only the no-sound of the woods. A Cooper's hawk flew overhead. A whitetail deer appeared about thirty feet away, looked down and chomped old remnants of green growth. I saw eyes deep brown as creek mud look at us, two pale human intruders in his space. He turned and immediately disappeared. A red-headed flicker poked its beak into a tree trunk. I watched all this with a settledness, a deepening ease, a seeping calm.

Then a ragged cough pulled itself up and out of my lungs. I held my fist to my mouth and my eyes watered as the cough exploded, loud and violent. When it eased, I exhaled and my body sagged. Noreen didn't look at me but I watched her as she stood. She smoothed the front of her expensive-looking jacket, tight around her pudgy middle and then dusted dry leaves off her jeans.

"Thanks for the smokes." I stood up. I reached down and picked up the brown book with its pages of wildflower pictures and notes. I flipped to a page near the front of the fat book. I tore out a page. On it, a picture of a happy cat sleeping in the sunshine.

"Would you take this to Dawson for me?"

Noreen nodded. "I know Lavinia would like him to have it, too."

I looked at the paper. As he grew, Dawson would see the cat and read the words I had written on the page. My thoughts, my handwriting, my sketches would help connect us. I felt myself exhale and somehow, as the air went out, I felt a sense of continuity, of a thread of ages-old comfort. But immediately, the overall bone-weariness returned.

"Good-bye, Ken," Noreen said, a sound of hard purpose in her voice. Then she said quietly, "I'm sorry." Or maybe it was just a whisper of pines rustling in a breeze.

"So long, Noreen." I looked at her and noticed her lips never parted as they pulled themselves taut across her face, like a curtain that's stretched across an empty stage. She intentionally moved her gaze from my face, over my tiny encampment and into the woods. I rubbed the still-puffy scar on my wrist and watched her stare straight ahead as her long-legged gait aimed her away from me. A prolonged ugly rattle sounded from deep inside me. She did not look back.

The next day, weakness felt fluid, washing a tide into my body. I rolled the sleeping bag and packed up. Altitude adjustment, that's all it was. I knew I needed to get farther into the forest and I'd be fine. My mind seemed to have trouble shifting gears. Food had lost its taste but I knew I needed protein so I chewed a handful of peanuts. I took a long drink of water from the bottle. I knew the harbor sage grouse were coming in for the winter and I might see golden eagles. I'd see moose and maybe a black bear and pronghorn. They'd all be looking for food, a way to ease themselves into the next season of life.

I knew I needed the woods around me, just like I needed them when I was a boy and Reggie and I were left. I need to pull the cloak of nature around me, need the warmth, the protection, the safety. I need the fragrance of the pines, of the juniper and wild grasses. I need the deepness of the woods, the changing of the seasons. I need the wildflowers of fading fall. I need the healing.

I rubbed my eyes with my knuckles. I can't think about Reggie. He's got a new life and he's happy now. That's what counts. I'll think about Dawson, about how I'll hold him and look into his happy future in his eyes. I'll think about how he will have love and family around him all his life.

I put my left arm through the backpack strap and swung the pack around so my right arm slid in. I heaved the pack up on my back, shrugged to adjust it. I tightened the strap that held it snug. The strap seemed to get longer every day and it flapped against my leg as though it was happy with its own uselessness.

Maybe Noreen is right; we each make our own decisions and maybe mine wrapped around the people in my life, maybe I wrapped myself around the axle. The ones I loved and lost, maybe those people didn't belong to me for all eternity in the first place. Maybe my job was just to forgive them, figure out how to let them go and live my life. I can't quite figure it out. Reggie and I helped each other grow up and we understood each other. With him so far away, there is no one who has known me and loved me my whole life, no one to help me remember my story, help me explain my story.

I dropped the cigarette butt to the ground and stomped out the glow with the heel of my hiking boot. I kicked up a little shelf of dirt with the toe of that same boot, nudged the cigarette into its final resting place and smoothed the dirt back down into a flat little mound. No one would notice it for a long, long time.

I loved Liv so much. And I did my best to be a good dad to her, to give her love and security and freedom. She named her baby Dawson, after me, my family name. I've held onto that thought and it warms me and fills me with hope. After a few more days hiking, I'll go see Liv and tell her how much joy she has ahead of her. I want her to know that no matter what has happened, my love for her is still there.

As I moved, I heard the sound of my hiking boots collapsing layers of paper-thin leaves, leaves whose falling signals decline.

Maybe Noreen is right, that things just happen in life. But jeeze, that sounds simplistic. And life isn't simple, it's complicated. All I know is I've done my best every day. I'll tell that to Dawson. And as he grows, I'll explain that his life will be different but it will have peaks and valleys. All lives do. I'll tell him not to let it sink in too deeply but to learn to forgive and to stay open no matter what. Yeah, that's what I'll do. I'll tell Dawson to keep breathing into his own life and keep finding the beauty and the fragrance in it.

I bent down to pick up the bags and winced as I felt the familiar burn in my chest, the ache in my knees, wrists and shoulders, the high-mileage joints. I divided the two slick white plastic shopping bags, and held one in each hand for balance. Each bag held precious cargo – cartons of cigarettes.

I am who I am – how could I have been a different man? Could I have done something, anything that would have made my mother stay? Could I have been a different husband to Noreen, a different father to Liv? I always felt a parent's love for her – should I have told her sooner that I'm not her biological dad? Would that have mattered? Did she know how much I always loved her? Noreen's probably right- things in life happened and I have to make peace with that. That's the work of life, the way the story unfolds and that's what I'll tell Dawson.

Livingstone was looking for the source of the Nile, that was his life's work. I thought my life's task was working on cars and taking care of them for people. But now I know my life's work has been to love and to forgive and to share what I've learned. If Dawson knows that, it will allow him to grow up stronger and to savor every experience. Now that I'm starting to know all this, see it like it's being revealed, and feel it in my soul, am I nearing the end of my journey? I shake my head. I can't think about that right now.

As I walk now, I think about getting to a comfortable spot in the woods. Years ago, the Arapahoe lived there because they felt the area had a spiritual sense, an atmosphere of connectedness, an air of resolution. I want the woods to surround me, fold me in, make my existence a part of their continuum. I want to go where the oxygen is clear and then maybe I can breathe and become a part of the universe.

I'm west of Rocky Mountain National Park now and the spot that straddles the Continental Divide isn't far. Timber Creek car camping area is nearby but I don't want to be around happy, busy families right now. I'll go a little farther and hollow out a little spot for myself. I straightened the backpack and with each step, felt its weight rub against the thinly fleshed bones of my back.

If I can get to Bowen Lake in Never Summers, I'll see some of the finest views in the Rockies - steep, rugged peaks and crystal clear streams with lush vegetation - and I'll feel better. The view of the woods, the mountaintops of fourteeners, the sky - it'll clear my mind and I'll be able to think straight, make some plans. Yeah, that'll make me feel better. I'll make a campsite and get comfortable. I'll plan on visiting Liv, I'll think about holding her baby and wondering what his life will be. I'll think about what springtime will look like. I can already picture it in my mind … true color, new blossoms, the cycle of life.

Now I've hiked over loose rock and scrim and I'm here at Chair Mountain. I am sitting on the old sleeping bag with my heavy jacket pulled tight around me. The cold seems to grow more prickly every minute. I glance at the white plastic sack that holds the last two cartons of cigarettes. I sit knees up, and feet flat on the ground, pressing into it. My elbows rest on my knees and my thin arms meet and fold to include each other. My left hand holds the right elbow in the crook between thumb and forefinger. My right hand is bent at the wrist and my thumb, index and middle fingers hold the red-embered cigarette.

I remember sitting almost exactly this way when I asked Daddy, "Why did Mama leave us?" But now my head is not bent, my back is not bowed under the pressing weight of unanswered questions. Now, over thirty years after I had questioned Daddy aloud, thirty years I had spent questioning myself silently, I know there are only fuzzy answers, answers that have morphed and changed with time and circumstance, answers that are never clear as sunshine. I feel now that I've dealt with each day, each eruption in nature's calm, the best way a man could.

When my mother left us, maybe it really had very little to do with me, very little to do with Daddy or Reggie either. She lived her own life and maybe none of us really knew who she was before she drove the old Plymouth out west. She left because of a bundle of wadded up needs she had toted around like candy wrappers stuffed in a glove compartment. Reggie and I could have been anybody, it probably wouldn't have mattered. Maybe she didn't leave us because she stopped loving us, maybe she just subtracted herself. We happened to be the remainders. I wonder if she had any idea how much Reggie and I hurt, how being left like that soaked like dye through the rest of our lives, how the sadness and self-doubt leached into every emotion we ever had.

And Noreen, maybe she was right that I tried to get a woman's love and approval in everything I did. And so what if I did? I was always good to Noreen. She complained I gave in too easily. I didn't want to be her doormat but I probably did give in. Reggie always said I was tense and jittery around Noreen, that I jumped at her every remark and moved immediately to meet her every command.

And it's true, I always felt like there was an oil puddle on the ground under me. I wanted our marriage to feel as fixed and old as the peaks – but it never did. It always felt like solid could be replaced by slippery at any minute; like things could shift and we could change into other people, people who barely knew each other. Maybe that's what being abandoned does to you, I don't know.

Noreen gave me some answers but some mysteries will always be cave-dark and completely unknown – that's just how life is. I couldn't fix my life the way I could fix a car, couldn't tinker with the pieces until the engine ran smoothly for myself and anybody else. Maybe boyhood is just a jumble, jigsaw pieces of the unknown, story pieces not made to fit together – maybe every childhood is, not just mine.

I think about how at Mac's Garage, we'd had a wooden crate filled with odd parts. As we worked on cars and trucks and even tractors, we'd find a worn out piece – a spark plug or a nut and bolt or a rusty spring - and we'd just toss it into the box. All those odd parts, tangled up together. Even if we took each piece out, wiped the greasy past off it, the bits wouldn't fit together, wouldn't create a whole anything. Is that the way life is?

I think that soon I'll go see Liv and her son. I'll tell him that it could be that life is a series of mysteries with all of us trying our best to love each other through it, each in our own imperfect way like two porcupines hugging.

That thought sinks deep into me and spreads itself out heavily. It occupies the space of my consciousness. I feel the skin around my eyes loosen, the tightness in my throat unknot. I feel I can pull my navel in toward my backbone and straighten myself as I inhale deeply and sense the sweetness.

I know now there were no answers to questions like 'Why did she leave me?' Could I have created a different life, an uncrushed life? Was there a way to protect myself or the ones I love from the chaos of life and hurt? How could I have reacted differently, been a different man? I know those questions would always be present, huge. But now they are no longer weigh on me like an engine block pressing down; now their edges are watery and runny with forgiveness. Knowing that no answers exist, that no amount of guilt can solve the past, that only acceptance for the imperfect allows me to move forward, shrinks the questions, paints them with opalescence, blurs the edges, dilutes their power.

I snub the cigarette out in the million-year-old former riverbed soil and my phlegm-filled, hacking cough falls over it like a rough, unwelcome blanket. I am skinny and the ash-grey skin I see in my small shaving mirror hangs loose like limp leaves on a cottonwood tree at the end of summer. My throat is tight and I am having trouble swallowing.

A story I had read in high school pops into my mind. Dr. Livingstone, the Scottish explorer whose name I knew from childhood, was exploring in Africa when a lion picked him up. The story was that the lion opened its huge jaws and clamped them around the explorer, and shook the man violently. Dr. Livingstone reported later that he felt he was going to die, knew that the lion would smash him against a rock or the ground until he was senseless, and then eat him. But miraculously, the lion got tired of the game and dropped the man. The scientist said later that when he was being shaken most violently, he had a sense of calm, a feeling of clearness, a view of saturated open white nothingness. At that moment when he thought he was going to die, he knew a sense of total peace and calm.

I am sitting slumped over and I notice mountain gentian and asters both blooming purple in the late fall air and I realize the cold has seeped into me. It reaches inside the jacket and spreads itself into every porous ounce of my thin body.

I shiver as I unzip the lined jacket, take it off and wearing worn jeans and faded flannel shirt, climb into the steady brown sleeping bag, my comfortable companion. Before I curl up, I spread the jacket out over the sleeping bag, trying to saturate extra warmth into my wasting body. I wish the jacket were Tooley, long dead now, lying soft and purry on my chest. In my mind, I see her whiskers twitching as she dreamed. I think about how she was named.

All four of us had gone to Mrs. Fullenweider's to see the new kittens. Reggie wanted the kitten with the odd pattern of black and brown spots and Mrs. Fullenweider said she'd be delighted for him to have it.

"We can't take her home today," Mama had told him. "She's just a baby and her eyes aren't even open yet. She needs some more time with her mom. We'll come back in a couple of weeks. Right now, she's just too little. But one day, she'll be ready to leave her mother and the other kitty babies."

"Too-lee-tle," Reggie had said. "Too-lee." And that's what we called her for sixteen years. Tooley had lived a long, happy life filled with love and adventure when she lay down under the cottonwood in the fading afternoon sun. The small boulder Reggie had placed on the spot where she was buried was still there.

A ragged, hard cough shakes my body and I feel the ache that accompanies it, feel the long-term trouble metastasizing up and rattling its way through my weak ribs and bony chest.

I lie on my back in the sleeping bag and while I look into the dimming late evening sky, I feel the edges of my mouth relax, ease downward, toward the earth. I feel the tension loosen in my face and I'm conscious that the wrinkle-lines of life have straightened themselves into a serene smoothness. As I relax, my face, even in the raincloud gray of my skin, feels like I am a boy again. Calm courses through my body like comforting liquid sun. My heart feels full, expanded, uplifted. Rounded white space, once filled with suspicion and question are now buoyed, lifted up by revelations, widened with realizations, expanded with confirmations and forgiveness. With a ragged, deep inhale, I breathe in the fragrance of the unknown all around me, above me, ahead of me.

Then a rattling, slowly exhaled breath causes me to tremble and my mind sees the conundrums of a lifetime float lazily upward on a pale gyre of light smoky cloud. I watch as the fading peach-colored rays of the sun turn to muted purple, puce and burnt orange - shades of bruises - as the dying day gives up its weight, abandons itself. When I feel I've seen it all, heavy lids slide down over my eyes and my body relaxes completely.

The night is deep and as I sleep, an unseasonable and unpredicted freezing, heavy-handed rain bears down on me, pushes on my heart. I wake myself as I cry out in my sleep, a beckoning that goes out to the cosmos. A chilling hollowness settles over me, into me, through me. Then there is a sudden vibrant warmth that blows the scent of the wild out of my body and into the never-ending swirl of the life force of the universe.

Acknowledgements

This novel began as a writing prompt, an article in the *Rocky Mountain News*, at a workshop led by the talented Annie Dawid at the Taos Summer Writers' Conference. During the five times I attended the conference, I was fortunate enough to study with contemporary greats Robert Boswell, Minrose Gwinn and Antonya Nelson. The conference was organized by the amazing Sharon Ord Warner, capably assisted by Eva Lipton-Ormond. I am grateful for the wonderful guidance and enriching experiences I had before TSWC was forced to close its doors in 2016.

I am also grateful to Lighthouse Writers' Workshop in Denver where I've benefitted from classes with William Heywood Henderson, Erika Krouse, Steve Almond and others. Andrea Dupree and Mike Henry and Laurie Wagner encouraged me, and hundreds of others, along the way.

Early on, I studied with Robin Black and will always be grateful for her skill and guidance and the intensity and focus she brings to writing. Thank you to the poet Ross White for connecting us.

Arline Dawson was one of my early and heart-warmingly encouraging readers and she and Phil have given me permission to use their name. Jan Ellison and Kathy Moss Bradford were also early readers as was my creative and dear writer-friend Roxanne Doty. I couldn't have put this together without the eagle-eyed reading by Gerry Pearson and Steve Pearson. My brother Doug Gregory is my go-to guy for details about cars. Heidi McNinch provided local information, color and great tours of the area described in the story. Amelia

Hurlburt and Katie Nolton shared their insights on the behavior of an upset teenage girl.

My father's mother left his family when he was a teenager and in spite of that, or because of it, he was a warm, witty, loving man. I'm eternally grateful to be his daughter. While this is his story, it also isn't – I made it up, the story and the characters are a work of fiction.

I give unending gratitude to my family for the warmth and love and support they infuse into my life every day and appreciation to my husband John who never stopped encouraging me and who loves me bettern' than chocolate chip cookies.

About the Author

photo credit: Wendy Smith Wood

ANDI GREGORY PEARSON is a fiction writer and her short stories, personal essays and book reviews have appeared in various publications. She grew up in the South and now lives in Golden, Colorado. This is her first novel.

www.andipearson.com